RETURN TO CALM

RETURN TO CALM

JACQUES RÉDA

TRANSLATED AND WITH AN INTRODUCTION BY
AARON PREVOTS

HOST PUBLICATIONS
AUSTIN, TX

Host Publications, Inc. 1000 East 7th, Suite 201, Austin, TX 78702

Layout and Design: Joe Bratcher & Anand Ramaswamy
Cover Art: Małgorzata Maj
Back Cover Photo: Jacques Sassier © Éditions Gallimard
Cover Design: Anand Ramaswamy

First Edition

Library of Congress Cataloging-in-Publication Data

Réda, Jacques, 1929-
  [Retour au calme. English]
  Return to calm / Jacques Réda ; translated and with an introduction by Aaron Prevots.
    p. cm.
  Summary: "An English translation of the French poetry collection Retour au calme"--Provided by publisher.
  ISBN-13: 978-0-924047-46-6 (hardcover : alk. paper)
  ISBN-10: 0-924047-46-1 (hardcover : alk. paper)
  ISBN-13: 978-0-924047-47-3 (pbk. : alk. paper)
  ISBN-10: 0-924047-47-X (pbk. : alk. paper)
  I. Prevots, Aaron. II. Title.
  PQ2678.E28R4813 2007
  841'.914--dc22
                              2007019822

TABLE OF CONTENTS

AUX PASSAGÈRES / TO SHORT-LIVED LOVES

NOUVELLES IMPRESSIONS FERROVIAIRES /
NEW RAILWAY IMPRESSIONS

L'AIR LIBRE / THE OPEN AIR

DEUX SAISONS PARISIENNES / TWO PARISIAN SEASONS

L'hiver des rues / The Winter of Streets

ÉCOLES DU SOIR / EVENING SCHOOLS

UN PARADIS D'OISEAUX / A PARADISE OF BIRDS

INTRODUCTION

[A]t the time I sported a fairly extraordinary pair of suspenders,
not terribly elastic frankly but, against a backdrop of night blue,
sown with tiny stars that seemed to raise me off the ground.
And, even though now I use like most a belt, redivided
every morning according to an order hardly new,
I've stayed floating between the coal and the stars.

> — Jacques Réda,
> "The Starred Suspenders"

Translating *Retour au calme* was a true pleasure because its poems
leave one "floating between the coal and the stars," raised up from
routine and better able to admire the beauty in the everyday, as in this
piece from the opening section where the speaker delights as much in a
diamond-like pile of coal by the riverbank as in his childhood
suspenders "sown with tiny stars." Jacques Réda has made a name for
himself in and beyond France because he combines this sharp eye for
the exact nature of all he observes with a thinker's soul (and lover's
melancholic heart) attuned to how people and things interact. In
Return to Calm he is a writer in motion, expansive in his portrayal of
days present and past. He holds a mirror up to ordinary events in an
effort to reveal their innate poetry, as if to ask, Does the world belong
to us or do we instead belong to it?

Before turning to *Return to Calm*'s intriguing mix of the lyrical
and the impersonal, of sensations and emotions conveyed in a quietly
rhythmical approach, there is first Réda's creative output to consider.
The author of numerous poetry collections, essays, short novels and
more difficult to classify books, Réda has for over forty years been an

active presence in French literature. Especially known for his explorations of places, urban as much as suburban, Parisian as much as European, he has also made a name for himself by ably switching between poetry and prose, depending on the subject matter and his inspiration of the moment. He has since the 1960s been a contributor to *Jazz Magazine* and published regularly with major editors such as Gallimard and Fata Morgana. Currently available in English are *The Ruins of Paris* and *Treading Lightly: Selected Poems 1961-1975*, the former a series of prose poems and the latter a regrouping of verse from the volumes *Amen*, *Récitatif*, and *La Tourne*. *Return to Calm* is the first full-length bilingual edition of one of Réda's books. In France, however, the depth and breadth of his vision, as well as his fluid style and deft touch, have won him important prizes since as early as 1969, for *Amen* (the *Prix Max-Jacob*), continuing on through to more recent awards including a *Grand Prix de l'Académie Française* (1993) and a *Prix Louis Mandin* (2005), both for his writings as a whole. French-language readers have been able to enjoy a steady stream of works appearing over the last few years, for example *Autobiographie du jazz* [*Autobiography of Jazz*] (Climats, 2002), *Ponts flottants* [*Floating Bridges*] (Gallimard, 2006) and *Toutes sortes de gens* [*All Sorts of People*] (Fata Morgana, 2007).

Beyond French shores, Réda may well be best known as a prose stylist whose sensitive evocations of life in and around Paris shed light on this city's endless fascination and mystery. Without necessarily aiming to reinvent iconic works such as Baudelaire's *Parisian Prowler* or *Parisian Tableaux*, he has done his own considerable share of city wandering and described it meticulously on many occasions. What one discovers in speaking with Réda, though, is his love of reading and writing themselves, and his desire to always hone his craft so that others will in their way want to accompany him. Indeed, a conversational thread, a touch of the familiar, runs throughout Réda's works: he knows his audience may be somewhat cynical, yet writes to maintain some of the flame-like intensity of works that shaped him, and seeks out strategies to convince the disabused. He thus favors gracefulness, sensitivity to detail, extended asides and a touch of wry, whimsical humor as a means to the end of recreating lived experience. Where Frenchness in literature so often connotes daring, boldness, devotion to originality and an experimental avant-garde, Réda instead favors measured steps, nonchalance, careful modesty and cautious appraisal. He seems particularly at home with essays having an autobiographical slant, yet has also enjoyed examining other writers, including Jorge Luis Borges, Charles-Albert Cingria and, in *La Sauvette* [*Quick Thoughts*], a wide range of poets. His writings on jazz, meanwhile, emphasize various musicians' personal and professional trajectories, as well as the ways they found to heed jazz's call for smooth, energetic swing.

In poetry, Réda's often long lines and attention to the pulse and flow that lend swing to writing make him a unique figure on the contemporary French literary horizon. Fashions come and go in any country's artistic traditions, and Réda associates himself unregrettingly with those of earlier eras and other centuries, particularly in terms of versification. With the unfolding of space and the passing of time as main topics in his verse, moreover, it seems only natural for him to do so. His poetry encourages a quiet faith of keeping watch, and his interest in rhyme adds an interesting twist to the blend of uncertainty and attentiveness that have characterized poetry in the last fifty years. Frequently on the lookout for deepened connections, he realizes they may remain at bay but encourages poems to emit slight signals of hope to us through the interplay of words on the page. Hints of emotion, particularly expressed as admiration for our natural surroundings, further point Réda's poetry toward the lyrical according to today's poetic compass. And yet, because his verse sways, almost as a wooden door in a light wind by the sea might, between opening onto celebratory moments and shutting tight against discoveries that don't quite happen, it can be hard to classify his work as falling squarely into any one stylistic camp. A better tack, then: looking to *Return to Calm* itself.

Return to Calm mostly does what it implies – it will soothe, reassure, suggest forgiveness, appease. Following as it does, especially for readers relying on English, on the more plaintive and urgent earlier works, it offers both a glimpse of what could be called Réda's middle period (1982-2002) and an overview of his poetic vision in several contexts. For example, there is always an individual describing events somewhat in the way of a narrator, along with memorable lines that make us feel the poet has tapped a vein of deep understanding: "Were we not already…to some / Sudden desire thrown to pasture, on the black / Pool table's cloth launched into the trajectories of spheres?" ("The Black Billiard Table"); "I was the hubs, spokes and rim of the / Accelerating wheel" ("Dark May"). But is *Return to Calm* metaphysical, or nature-centered, or poetry of travel or of the city or of self-awareness? All of the above, with rhythmic twists and imagistic touches in which we recognize Réda's voice. In and of themselves, the seven section titles highlight the mix of perspectives and the range of topics to be addressed. We move from memories that leave the speaker "empty-handed"; to reflections on youth and "short-lived loves"; to vignettes in which an eye is cast on journeys in the "open air"; to a focus on Parisian seasons and the here and now closer to home. Occasional refrains such as "it's spring" lend wistfulness to this vision, while winter poems such as "The Thaw" suggest that time and space, left to their own devices, remain disinterested in the human realm of immediate thought and action and are poised to remember no more than instants, always "the same," that pass.

To some extent, Réda makes it clear that the speaker in his poems is caught up in uncontrollable processes, floating in a universe hardly of personal design and which inevitably is contemplated with some bemusement. Singular in this respect, and hopefully not too surprising for Anglophones, is the frequent use of the pronoun "on," translated for the most part here as "one," with occasional switches especially when capturing a more casual spoken tone was necessary. Though such French tics may feel quite normal to some, especially to fans of Rimbaud's famous letters aware that language 'thinks us,' Réda applies this aspect of everyday speech fairly liberally, to emphasize situations where the speaker could be standing in for any poet or person immersed in things seen and felt. A touching example of this occurs in "The Bakery," where "one sees the bread / Circle with gold the shopgirl's curly hair," in this local shop that glows "for the sole glory / Of bread." In the French, "one" sees this near-sacred scene and "one" can't help but "give thanks" for its light. This somewhat impersonal aspect of Réda's writing meshes with the frequent and curious reversals wherein things in the world are doted with a conscience, as in "Cedar at Meudon" when "One suspects" that the villas "with loose flapping shutters" "know, standing on their philosopher's bank, / Why the night approaches in small bounds at the valley's flank." Also noteworthy with respect to French phrasing is the relative economy that characterizes Réda's poetry, with the lines of roughly twelve to fifteen syllables typically fitting in balanced form a series of statements, as if an actual listener were already present when they took shape.

It would be hard not to conclude this introduction without mention of Réda's love affair with the world around him and the occasional wry humor that surfaces as he writes. The blend of almost contradictory impulses and images appears to strong effect in the last of his "Four Seascapes," where "The cold, horizontal world…doesn't know it's ours and beautiful." Especially eloquent are the "Paradise of Birds" poems, where a "murky riot" of cries ("Poetry") quite distracts the speaker each morning yet also is capable of transforming "all space into a diamond resonating sweetly / Crossing its fires in time's motionless heart" ("A Paradise of Birds"). At the opposite end of this spectrum are, for instance, "By Leroy's Place" and "The Price of Time at the Île Saint-Germain." In the latter, the result of the speaker's "pact" with a passer-by is not the time requested in exchange for a bit of small change (the passer-by has no watch), but rather an "oblique / Shadow" seen afterward that is "true and melacholic." In the former, an almost surreal farmyard scene reveals "a bit of laundry not how it should / Be raised in an equivocal gesture of welcome." *Return to Calm* makes us feel a fascination for our surroundings, no matter the unexpected ways in which they present themselves to us.

Réda's poetry also provides a window on his prose, where his uniquely light touch speaks to the senses and likewise makes for an experience at once enjoyable and profound. His style both sings through its rhymes, phrasing and images and swings (in the manner of America's saxophone greats) through its rhythms, detours and asides. Whether quietly murmured or marked by a certain playfulness and warmth, *Return to Calm* uplifts and entrances, as much through its thoughtful seeking and questioning as through its striking, yet in their images so recognizable, I-wish-I-had-said-that lines.

Aaron Prevots
Southwestern University
Georgetown, Texas

FROM JACQUES RÉDA

I should first beg the reader's forgiveness for offering these reflections on writing and on my development as a writer in English, or perhaps I should say "my" English, and for using "I" as well while laying little claim to any particular reputation in America, certainly not as a literary critic or doctor or theoretician, yet nonetheless happy to introduce myself to an audience there. It was only through the encouragement of first Andrew Shields and then Aaron Prevots, both fellow translators, that I felt reasonably comfortable setting down my thoughts in this way. Indeed, it isn't a language I ever learned very seriously, even in school between ten and seventeen, and in general was acquired mostly from the liner notes of jazz LPs and the titles and lyrics of tunes sung by Ella Fitzgerald, Billie Holiday, Louis Armstrong, Mose Allison, Fats Waller or Nat King Cole. I traveled several times in England, Ireland and Scotland, but all in all spent only a week in the United States – in and around San Francisco. I'm told that wasn't really and truly America, nor New Orleans and New York, so I'm planning my next trip, God willing, to be in Arkansas or Oklahoma. My America is an imaginary one, built up from the comics I read when I was a boy and, later (after World War II), from films, and above all from novels by Faulkner, Hemingway, Steinbeck, Caldwell, Saroyan, Salinger and so on. In this respect, I'm not so unusual but rather quite representative of my generation.

My taste for jazz was itself common among teenagers in those times, but few of us stuck to it, got wider and deeper in their acquaintance with it as I did, year after year, so much so that I'm now the oldest contributor to the French monthly *Jazz Magazine*, besides having published three books on the subject, quite uncommon among writers. No doubt I'm an impressionistic or, shall we say, "philosophical" analyst rather than a true musical one, and thus have the misfortune of being considered a dreamer by musicians and a bore by those possibly interested in my other works. Moreover, I always took good care to disappoint those too quick to find something overtly jazzy in my way of writing.

As sure as one can be that rhythm is a basic element in every kind of language, I'm equally convinced English is the only tongue where natural tonic accents have a relation to what in jazz is called *swing*, a merely musical phenomenon closely connected to voice and singing. You won't find it in French prosody (either verse or prose), although I've been unwise enough, even though I specifically said it was a simile, to relate our mute e to the idea of a kind of syncopated note.

I'm dwelling on the subject to correct the first image I gave of "my" America: jazz is not an imaginary fact, but jazz is also not the whole of America. During the summer preceding my ears' initiation, mostly unaided by the hymns and anthems of the Latin (Gregorian) Catholic liturgy, I'd listened to a quite different (yet percussive) type of American music, played by the U.S. Air Force and artillery. I really stood quite close to death when bombed by two hedge-hopping "Lightning P-38s." I must admit, however, that the marks under the wings were Canadian. *And that*, to quote Robert Frost, *has made all the difference*, for, two weeks later, applauded, as you can imagine, and by no means imaginary, the first Americans I had met until then appeared. Unfortunately, one of them was killed by a German a few yards from my home. I was fifteen, he was nineteen, and from where he came I don't know but I never forgot his name: Elmo Penton, and you might find him living in some of my poems as a trace of a real America.

Did I write poems by that time? Most definitely: it was only the start of a period which lasted about ten years more, and I used to describe it as my "parrot period." My only reference was the schoolbook entitled *Morceaux choisis pour les lycées et collèges* [*Selected Works for Middle and High Schools*], from which I took all my raw material. If I read Villon, I wrote ballads; Ronsard, I wrote sonnets. Racine? I plunged for twenty verses into the soul of a Roman emperor in love. La Fontaine? At once, a dialogue between a horse and a wasp was born. Lamartine? I besought Time to cease its flight. Rimbaud? I was illuminated. My secret copybooks look like a flea market where crooked copies of antiques and not so modern furniture were piled up day after day, in no real order. What was I searching for but myself? And there wasn't a single shadow of my own between 1044 and 1944: nine centuries of French poetry rewritten for nothing! When afterwards some more consistent shadows began to prowl across this gallery of illusions, I found them so weak I gave up. But mighty indeed is the demon of literature, and I tried for years to write novels and short stories. I had no precise models in mind, and generally succeeded in writing the first two or three chapters of my masterpiece. After I grew weary of my characters, I always found myself unable to straighten out their problems.

Thus things proceeded until 1960, of which the final zero is significant. I fell deep into the well opened by its circumference. Then, one morning in 1961, I can't say why I emerged out of the hole, but I know how: pulled out by six or seven lines I scrawled on a scrap of paper as if I'd made a copy, but without an original. Without having read anything like it elsewhere, and nonetheless it was exactly *that which I sought*. And that which I sought and thus found was not a sudden, dazzling betrayal of a hidden ability. *That which I sought* had come through from what the Ancients call a Muse or, more abstractly, inspiration, and the Moderns would identify with a famous phrase from Rimbaud, saying *I is an other*.

It should also be stated that this mental experience is by no means a witness of its properly poetic outcomes. I am not hinting at a favor a God would have bestowed upon me. And why would any consider doing so, if not for my sluggish doggedness of purpose? Which would have hardly been stirring. I think this experience shows how essential the part of dispossession of oneself is in the act of writing, and the idea is everything you might want it to be, except new, so it doesn't seem too wrong to me.

Who then holds the pen or taps on a keyboard? I can now readily answer: language. Regarding poetry, I ultimately considered language basic and perhaps sufficient. Saying *cherry, cloud, squirrel, I'm tired* or *How do you do?* is already poetry and poems, and this is how I understand what Hölderlin said: *Man dwells as poet.* What of the poets who are, so to speak, "professionals"? With the same words used in everyday life, they try to make a "hyper-poetry" where most of them, including the author of these lines, are bested by vertigo, unless they wisely shun a glimpse from the beetling heights and sometimes dance graciously on the brink, where another God may keep them safe. Quite rare are those who can dance out over the brink and make the yawning chasm below perceptible: here and there Marot (1496-1544) and Toulet (1867-1920). The latter is one of my greatest ideals, though he wrote few poems. Take for example the following stanzas from *Les Contrerimes* [*Counter-Rhymes*]:

Dying, too, is not a shadow:
If ever you take fright,
Don't listen to your heart at night,
It is a queer sorrow.

And translation itself? In some cases, we might rather call it naturalization. It is true that a primary part of poetry's soul lies in the very flesh of its words insofar as they are a matter of sensual delight, but the emphasis of a poem depends on its theme, ideas and images as much as on its euphonic properties, its sounds. And the paradox is, whereas music as pure music is allegedly accessible to everyone, the musical part of tongues, somewhat hesitating between greediness and mysticism, seems reluctant to spread beyond its natural borders. Is it not however a matter of care, time – and love? I spent many hours reading Dante or Borges with translations and the original side by side, and is it a mere illusion if I think I have, in the long run, caught something of their elusive melody?

In this respect, there is also the example of Paul Valéry, and his view of poetry as "a symbiosis of sense and sound." For various reasons,

Valéry's prosody eventually appeared to be a hopeless renewal, or a last flaming, of forms brought to perfection by La Fontaine and Racine. As for myself, I always stood on the fringe of literary cliques and polemics, seeking only the best way to express what I felt, which had to be said now in prose, now in verse, sometimes in free verse, sometimes in classic ones, but in the latter case having every respect for the rules. So I might be, in my generation, one of the rare poetic animals sensitive to Valéry's consummate art, and one who is pleased to use, as often as necessary, old tools in handiworks he has in view, if they are suitable to them. The French (Swiss-born) contemporary writer I praise the most highly, Charles-Albert Cingria (1833-1954), thought poetry was a craftsman's knack backed up by an astral beam. Maybe a small spark of it struck my brain on that day in 1961. Some of the greatest poets have been burnt to death by that beam; to others, it supplied an energy stored and transformed in the high-voltage current that ran through their being and still runs through their prose. When reading them, or those of less electrifying power (sometimes you need a light turned low), I'm plugged in and don't want to know who writes, who reads – reading being, *for the present*, to quote Borges, *an act subsequent to writing: more resigned, more urbane, more intellectual* and, I might add, often more exciting.

I may have inherited this feeling from my "parrot period." When someone asks me which author had a determinative effect on me, I answer: everyone, including railroad timetables. It should be no wonder if one of the main occupations in my life until now has been reading manuscripts and, for eight years (one hundred issues), editing a well-known French literary review where I published some of the best poets and novelists of various generations. As for my own writing, I don't like to look back, and always endeavor to go forth, not unaware that, whatever the beam's strength may be, it illuminates an inner space that can't be boundlessly stretched. But the search for new routes across it is possible and tempting, and in this way I contrived for years and years, through a combination of trains and a light motorbike, to roam about the limited yet so wonderfully various inner space of France, with an exultation never lessened by heat, frost, rain, flat tires or spills. Of which bear witness several of my wandering books, verse or prose, according to my mood, as well as some of the recollections you will find grouped together in the present bilingual pages.

RETURN TO CALM

LES MAINS VIDES

EMPTY-HANDED

LE BILLARD NOIR

Entre deux profondeurs de sommeil et d'oubli,
La terre tourne, et ferme, et rouvre son oeil bleu.
Notre état naturel est d'absence dans ces ténèbres.
Mais sans fin convoqués nous franchissons par vagues
L'espace que nos cils cernent ici dans l'épaisseur
Qui nous berce et nous abandonne. Morts. Normalement
Morts (sauf pour ce coup d'oeil rapide et circulaire), car
N'étions-nous pas déjà des morts avant de naître, à quel
Désir soudain jetés en pâture, et sur le drap
Du billard noir lancés dans les trajectoires des sphères?

THE BLACK BILLIARD TABLE

Between two depths of forgetting and sleep,
The earth turns, closes, reopens its blue eye.
Our natural state is of absence in these shadows.
But, endlessly summoned, in waves we cross the space
Our eyelashes outline here in the thickness
Which cradles and abandons us. Dead. Normally
Dead (this rapid, circular glance excepted), for
Were we not already dead before being born, to some
Sudden desire thrown to pasture, on the black
Pool table's cloth launched into the trajectories of spheres?

LE RETOUR DU BAL

Les vieux pères en habits raides,
Ils ont aussi franchi la porte, un soir d'été
Et, le temps d'une abeille,
La petite flamme immortelle
A dansé dans leurs yeux.
Tard dans la nuit, en revenant du bal,
Ils ont pissé dans le canal,
Contre le mur du cimetière,
Et du silence autour fort comme une montagne,
Descendait le torrent de soie des peupliers.
Déjà beaucoup de morts étaient en travail sous la terre,
Mais dimanche et l'oubli même les apaisaient,
Et la herse à l'envers au bout d'un champ luisait,
Tenant entre ses dents du foin mêlé d'étoiles.
À mi-côte ils ont appelé :
Pour rien, pour le plaisir d'entendre
Leurs voix se perdre au fond des granges, des greniers
Remplis d'un blé houleux comme le corps des femmes,
Et puis dans la rumeur toujours en marche sous la nuit.

THE RETURN FROM THE DANCE HALL

The old fathers in stiff clothes,
They too, one summer's evening, passed through the door,
And the small immortal flame
In bee time
Danced in their eyes.
Late at night, returning from the dance hall,
They pissed in the canal
Against the cemetery wall,
And from the surrounding silence strong as a mountain
Fell the poplars' torrent of silk.
Already many dead were at work under the earth,
But with Sunday and even forgetting they were calmed,
And the overturned harrow at a field's edge gleamed,
Holding between its teeth hay mixed with stars.
They called out at the hill's halfmark:
For no reason, for pleasure, to hear
Their voices lost deep within lofts
Filled with wheat turbulent as women's bodies,
In the rumor busily running, as always, under the night.

LA RENCONTRE

Le temps vint à pas de soleil sous les arbres, comme un nuage,
À peine un souffle dans le cou des enfants qui jouaient. Quel âge
Avions-nous donc? Je ne sais plus. Nous nous sommes levés
Pour le suivre, et j'ai vu couler la rivière.

THE ENCOUNTER

Time came at a sun's pace under the trees, like a cloud,
Barely a breath at the necks of the children playing. How old
Were we? I hardly know. We got up
To follow it, and I saw the river flow.

LES PREMIERS SIGNES

Parfois nous revient une odeur de colle, de plumier.
Alors le mol éclatement des bogues dans la cour
Fait signe encore au fond d'un jour presque oublié d'octobre
Où l'on a su qu'on n'était rien, déjà, qu'un souvenir.

THE FIRST SIGNS

Sometimes it comes back to us, a smell of pencil boxes, of glue.
Then the soft bursting of the husks in the courtyard
Still beckons from within a near-forgotten October day
When one first knew one was nothing, already, but a memory.

LA MAISON ROUGE

LA VISITE

Par un novembre obscur englouti sous les feuilles mortes
Qu'on amasse en marchant pour en mâcher l'odeur
(Et ma mère disait : tu vas abîmer tes chaussures,
Et mon père comme toujours ne disait pas un mot),
Au bout d'une avenue déserte où l'unique repère
Était, brune et rose, une usine de cacao,
Un dimanche on alla visiter la nouvelle maison.
Elle était haute et rouge, en brique avec des coins de pierre,
Pareille au château d'un poème étrange que j'avais lu,
Mais château de banlieue où devait pourrir ma jeunesse,
Comme entravé dans son étable un bouc irrésolu.
Et, dignement, avant les allées venues machinales,
Les éclats par-dessus la rampe et les portes claquant,
On remonta, redescendit l'escalier en spirale
Qui s'enfonçait jusqu'au sous-sol vers un jardin étroit.
Je m'émerveillai d'y trouver, tout au long de l'allée,
Si tardives et parfumées, quelques fraises des bois.
Sur le mur courait une vigne, et la grille rouillée
Donnait sur la berge du fleuve. On le sentait de loin
Qui roulait dans l'air mou d'automne un remugle de vase;
On entendait rire et glousser au fil de ses remous
Son corps abandonné hâtif à des lueurs sournoises.
En face, une île toute en prés avec un pavillon
Un peu chinois et malfaisant comme le lieu du crime
Et, sur de forts appontements épaissis de bitume,
Un peu plus loin le pont roulant d'un hangar à charbon.
Muet à ce moment sous les arbres sourds et la brume

THE RED HOUSE

THE VISIT

On a dark November swallowed up under the autumn leaves
That one gathers while walking to drink in the warm smell
(And mother would tell me: you'll ruin your shoes,
And father as usual said not a word),
At the end of a deserted avenue where there stood
A pink and brown cocoa factory, the sole landmark,
We went one Sunday to visit the new house.
It was tall, red, in brick edged with stone,
Just like a castle I'd read of in a strange poem,
But a suburban brick castle where my youth would go to rot
Like an indecisive billy goat blocked in its stable.
And, with much dignity, before the mechanical back and forth,
The shouting above the ramp and the closing of doors,
We climbed up and down the spiral staircase
That sank as far as the basement toward a narrow garden.
To my delight I found there, the whole length of the walk,
A few wild strawberries, sweet smelling, blooming late.
On the wall ran a vine, and the rusted railing
Looked out over the riverbank. One felt the river
Even from a distance, trundling in in the soft autumn air
Its moldy must like an overlooked vase; one heard
Its hasty abandoned body with its shifty gleam
Chuckle and laugh with each passing slap on the banks.
Across the way, an isle all meadows, a somewhat
Chinese-style pavilion, evil as a crime scene
And, on heavy wharves thickened with asphalt,
Further down a coal warehouse and its traveling crane.

(Mais j'allais aimer la douceur rauque de sa chanson),
Sur la sauvagerie à villas, entrepôts, légumes,
Il s'élevait comme un signal dans l'entre chien et loup,
La nuit tombant sur mon enfance – et je devinais tout.

Silent just then under the deaf trees and the fog
(Though I would learn to love the husky gentleness of its song),
On the wild scattered mix of villas, entrepôts, foods,
In the shadows of dusk it rose like a signal,
Night falling on my childhood – and I foresaw all.

MAI SOMBRE

Tout au fond du jardin chantait l'araignée à fourrure
Et le soleil de mai tissait sa toile sur les eaux.
J'écoutais le trop-plein de bleu brûler dans les orties
Et le souffle animal d'une locomotive
Veiller sur la solitude des dieux.
Alors en haut d'un arbre ou dans l'ombre d'un mur,
Je fus le moyeu, les rayons et le bord de la roue
Accélérant.
Et si c'est un malheur de vivre, il est moins grand
Pour qui dure en vieux mur de mousse sous les nuages,
Ouvrant toujours sa cavité sombre au soleil de mai
Nerveux comme un tueur entre le fleuve et le sentier;
Ombrageant des fleurs dont la tige aérienne prolonge
Une jambe de ciel ou d'enfant dans l'abricotier
Qui dérive à présent loin des jardins, loin des nuages.

DARK MAY

At the garden's far end the furry spider sang
And the May sun spun its web on the water.
I listened to the surfeit of blue burn in the nettles
And a locomotive's animal breath
Keep watch over the gods' solitude.
Then from above a tree or within a wall's shadow,
I was the hub, spokes and rim of the
Accelerating wheel.
And if living is unhappiness, one feels it less
When lasting like an old moss wall under the clouds,
Always opening to the May sun one's dark cavity
Nervous as a killer between the river and the path;
Shading flowers whose sylphlike stem prolongs
A sky-leg or child's leg in the apricot tree
Which drifts now far from the gardens, far from the clouds.

LES BRETELLES ÉTOILÉES

Il y eut quand même des matins où, je ne peux pas dire,
même en hiver, mais enfin surtout au printemps, l'été
(sans oublier l'automne dont le déclin est apothéose),
oui, des matins où tout allait pour de bon commencer.
Quand je dis tout, c'est tout. Il faut donc entendre: le monde
entier de partout jaillissant en tous sens comme une onde
ou comme une fille les poings aux hanches et rieuse: me voici.
Non que le monde n'eût pas existé la veille, l'avant-veille,
ou pendant les jours innombrables qui m'avaient précédé,
mais (et l'on s'expliquait alors une certaine distance,
une certaine incapacité de confiance ou de ferveur),
il y était resté pris sous la pure transparence
d'une très fine pellicule collant si juste à ses contours,
qu'on pouvait la plupart du temps omettre sa présence
comme celle du papier peint à fleurs dans la salle à manger.
On vivait cependant, mais comme sur la scène d'un théâtre
au décor circulaire planté pour l'ornement des jours,
pour une illusion de profondeur derrière les pensées et les êtres
non moins étroitement enfermés sur eux-mêmes tels des sourds.
Puis un matin l'enveloppe s'étant tout à coup déchirée,
on découvrait la vérité des formes, des couleurs.
Quelque chose remuait au fond du décor immobile
et, léger lambeau d'air plus tiède dans l'air, on était
traversé par les chants d'oiseaux hachés comme de la paille,
par les étincelles du fleuve et ses buissons d'odeurs.
Et chaque pas heurtait une corde tendue à se rompre,
fil soyeux de la trame qui tout entière alors vibrait
à la fois jusqu'au ciel dans l'écho d'un cristal sans voûte
et par tout l'espace de la terre en route dans sa grandeur.

THE STARRED SUSPENDERS

Still there were mornings where, I can't quite say,
even in winter, but at any rate especially in spring, summer
(not to mention autumn, its decline truly supreme),
yes mornings where everything was about to definitely begin.
When I say everything, that's everything. Meaning: the entire
world everywhere in all directions gushing forth, like a wave
or a girl with her fists on her hips laughing: here I am, it's me.
Not that the world didn't exist
the day before, the day before that, or
the countless prior days that had preceded me,
but (and one attributed then a certain distance,
a certain incapacity for fervor or confidence),
it had remained set there under the pure transparency
of a thin film clinging so right to its contours,
that one could most of the time miss out its presence
much as in the dining room that of the flowered wallpaper.
We nonetheless lived, but as if on a theater stage
with circular décor planted to adorn the days,
for an illusion of depth behind thoughts and beings
no less narrowly closed in on themselves as if deaf.
Then one morning with the tear of the membrane's cover,
one discovered the truth of colors, of forms.
Something stirred deep within the motionless decor
and, a light scrap of air milder in the air, one was
traversed by the birdsong itself cut up like straw,
by the sparks of the river and its bushes of smells.
And each step came against a string stretched to breaking,
the silky thread of the weft then vibrating altogether
both as far as the sky in an unvaulted crystal's echo

Le plus beau, quand j'allais ainsi le long des berges,
c'était, près du débarcadère, les gros tas de charbon
brillant comme du diamant au-dessus de leur barricade en poutres,
et plus loin cette petite manufacture de chocolat
si rose, parfumant l'air avec sa cheminée de tôle
droite sous la colline où moussait l'écume des lilas.
La lumière dorait les entrailles noires de la planète,
et dans ma tête la corde vibrait bien au-delà des mers.
Je percevais même sans bouger le changement, la vitesse;
les pylônes électriques à vastes enjambées passaient
en chantonnant d'un hémisphère à l'autre, et d'un moment
à l'autre on allait arriver mais partir. Je me rappelle :
en ce temps-là j'arborais d'assez extraordinaires bretelles,
pas très élastiques à vrai dire mais, sur un fond bleu nuit,
semées de minuscules étoiles qui semblaient me soulever de terre.
Et, bien que j'utilise à présent comme beaucoup une ceinture
qui tous les matins me repartage suivant l'ordre établi,
je suis resté flottant entre le charbon et les étoiles.

and over the whole of the earth's space underway in its greatness.
Most beautiful of all, when I'd walk thus along the banks,
was, near the landing dock, the huge pile of coal
shining like diamond above their barricade made of beams,
and further on this marvelously pink small chocolate
factory, perfuming the air with its sheet steel chimneystack
straight under the hill where the lilac's froth foamed.
The light gilded the planet's black entrails,
and in my head the string vibrated well beyond the seas.
Even without moving I sensed change and speed;
with vast strides the electric pylons passed
humming from hemisphere to hemisphere, from one moment
to the next one was about to get there but leave. I remember:
at the time I sported a fairly extraordinary pair of suspenders,
not terribly elastic frankly but, against a backdrop of night blue,
sown with tiny stars that seemed to raise me off the ground.
And, though now I use like most a belt, redivided
every morning according to an order hardly new,
I've stayed floating between the coal and the stars.

LA VIE ACTIVE

À l'aurore l'embrasement sur les verrières
Écoeurant la pâleur brutale des trottoirs,
J'éteignais et j'apercevais en bas les arbres noirs
Se ranger comme des fourgons pleins de nuit prisonnière
Le long des murs méchants qui rapetissent. Car
Le jour éclate et n'arrête plus jusqu'au soir
De grandir en tremblant de chagrin sur ses pattes,
Avant d'aller claquer tout seul au fond des squares
Qu'il remplit d'une extase louche et d'étincelles.
Je me souviens de la bonté des jardins en ficelle,
Des chemises gesticulant au bord des rails
Quand la maison du coin, happée en l'air par sa lanterne
Avec son attirail de clapiers et de matelas,
Volait sur les chantiers de démolitions et ténèbres.
Bon temps. Belle jeunesse. Et la douce étape du soir
Entre l'usine, l'autobus, l'amour et les paires de claques,
Où regardant crever les bulles dans la mousse
De la bière, je croyais voir
Le grand fond bouillonner sur le zinc des comptoirs.

THE ACTIVE LIFE

At dawn the blazing up against glass
Sickening the sidewalk's brutal pallor,
I'd switch the lights off and notice the black trees below
Line up like wagons full of night taken prisoner
Along the mean walls that get smaller. For
The day breaks out and till evening can be seen
Growing bigger trembling with sadness on its paws,
Before collapsing dead far back alone
In public squares, filling them with dubious ecstasy and sparks.
I remember the gardens roped with string, their kindness,
The gesticulating shirts at the railroad tracks' edge,
When the corner house with its jumble of hutches
And beds, snapped up into the air by its lantern,
Flew along the sites of demolitions and shadows.
Good times. Happy youth. And the gentle part of evening
Between the factory, the bus, love and the several smacks,
Where watching the bubbles in the beer-foam
Die out, I felt I was seeing the great backdrop
On the zinc of the countertops bubble up.

LA VIE DE FAMILLE

Voici : les deux pièces donnaient, par des portes vitrées,
Sur un couloir plus sombre et, dans l'une, je m'enfournais
Pour remplir et pour raturer ensuite ces carnets
Où l'énigme et quelques lueurs restaient enchevêtrées.
Cependant je recommençais avec une fureur
Muette qui pouvait aussi déchirer le silence
Et provoquait autour de moi la même vigilance
Anxieuse qu'auprès d'un grand malade. La terreur
Régnait ainsi le jour où, perdu dans cette tornade,
Inerte qui figeait mes élans comme ceux d'un fou —
Voire, plus simplement, d'un égoïste qui se fout
De tout — je vis les deux enfants, retour de promenade,
Poser contre la vitre la plus basse un nez tout rond,
Voulant entrer, me raconter leurs jeux, vaille que vaille.
Et je les ai laissés dehors (allons, papa travaille),
Et pleurer, partir. Maintenant, je sais qu'ils n'entreront
Plus jamais, alors que ce fut le seul moment peut-être
Où j'aurais pu, sans cette rage absurde, les sauver
De la rage du temps et, d'un geste, les enlever
Dans le ciel qui me surveillait à travers la fenêtre.

FAMILY LIFE

It was like this: through glass doors the two rooms opened
Onto a darker hallway and in one I closed
Myself in, dove into my notebooks and noted and altered
The enigma and the odd glimmer that lay tangled.
Yet I'd begin again with a furor
Gone mute that could also tear the silence
And that provoked around me the same vigilance
Gone anxious one offers the truly ill. Terror
Reigned thus the day when, lost in this whirlwind storm
Gone lifeless that froze me like a madman and his stare –
If not quite simply an egotist who couldn't care
Less – I saw the two children, returning in good form,
Place against the windowpane a nose all round,
Wanting to come in, tell me about their games somehow.
And I left them outside (go on, daddy's working now),
Let them cry and go away. Now I know without a doubt
They'll never come in again, whereas it was the one time I'd be,
Perhaps, if not for this absurd rage, poised
To save them from the rage of time and lift
Them with a gesture into the sky at the window watching me.

LA MAISON MORTE

La barrière à présent reste ouverte, car on n'a plus
Le courage de faucher l'herbe après les grosses pluies,
Quand s'élève en été cette tendre buée
Qui fait croire au retour des jours heureux d'autrefois.
Et ceux qui passent sur la route et voient, en contrebas,
Cette maison de brique et l'arbre aux figues déjà bleues,
Le seuil terreux où l'herbe en vagues molles vient rouler,
Pensent que le bonheur serait de vivre là longtemps,
Toujours, peut-être, au creux des nuages et des prairies :
Une maison pour une vie, à l'abri des coteaux
Et du ciel jamais indifférent qui va
D'un bord à l'autre avec la hâte raisonnée
D'une femme sachant le bon emploi de sa journée
Dans l'odeur de cire, de figue, et jusqu'au miel profond du soir.
Mais lui, qu'en pense-t-il, qui n'a pas remplacé
Le carreau du grenier cassé depuis un jour d'hiver
Déjà lointain, ni les rideaux sales, ni la serrure
Du cellier dont la porte bée et l'on voit un éclat
D'outils à l'abandon brillant même les nuits sans lune?
La cuisine, c'est là qu'il se tient d'habitude,
Accomplissant des gestes rares et machinaux.
Et sa pensée : un simple écho machinal de chaque geste,
Puisque rien ne peut arriver qui vaille encore un mot,
Un pas dans l'escalier tournant jusqu'à des chambres sans mémoire.
Plus personne n'habite ici, personne ne chuchote au fond
De l'eau qui va bouillir, ni dans le grincement des portes,
Avec le vent brassant des feuilles mortes sur le toit.
Le balancier terni de l'horloge qui tousse
Avant de sonner, vous saisit dans son va-et-vient comme un ours

THE DEAD HOUSE

The gate stays open now, for one no longer has
The courage to cut the grass after the heavy rains,
In summer when this tender fog rises
That brings back hope the happy days of yesteryear will return
And those who pass by on the road and see, looking down,
This brick house and the tree with its figs already blue,
The earthy threshold where the grass in soft waves rolls,
Think it would be sure happiness to live there a good while,
Forever, perhaps, in the hollow between the prairies and the clouds:
A house for a lifetime, sheltered from the hills
And from the never indifferent sky
That goes from one side to the other
With the reasoned haste of a woman
Who knows quite well how to spend her day
Amid the smell of wax, of figs, till the deep honey of evening.
But him, what does he think of all this, who hasn't replaced
The attic pane broken since a long gone
Winter's day, nor the dirty drapes nor the cellar lock
Where the door gapes and one sees the neglected tools'
Stray pieces that shine even on moonless nights?
The kitchen, that's where he usually stands,
Carrying out rare, mechanical gestures.
And his thoughts: of each gesture a mere mechanical echo,
Since nothing can happen worth the effort of a word,
A step down the spiral staircase to memoryless rooms.
No one lives here any longer, no one whispers
Within the water set to boil, nor in the creaking of doors,
With the wind on the rooftop stirring the dead leaves.
The tarnished pendulum of the clock that coughs

Solitaire qui s'étourdit contre le soleil froid.
Il y a pourtant des moments encore imprévisibles,
Ainsi lorsque sans réfléchir on retourne s'asseoir
Devant le lourd déferlement d'herbe qui se soulève
Et creuse des tunnels dorés où le soleil du soir
Promène une lanterne rose, et qu'il semble possible
De se souvenir prudemment, sinon d'espérer, en tout cas
De répondre au salut de ceux qui passent là-haut sur la route
    en pleine lumière.

Before ringing, in its back and forth grabs you like a solitary
Bear deadening its senses against the cold sun.
Yet there are moments still unpredictable,
As when without thinking it through one returns to sit
In front of the heavy surge of grass that swells
And digs gilded tunnels where the evening sun
Trails a pink lamp, and when it seems possible
To prudently remember, if not to hope, in any case
To respond to the greeting of those who pass above on the road
    immersed in light.

DÉMÉNAGEMENT

Il y a beaucoup à faire encore. Beaucoup. Trop. Il y a trop à faire.

Les trois quarts des bagages ne sont même pas bouclés

et, d'entre les mâchoires grandes ouvertes des valises,

reflue un désordre écoeurant de vêtements et d'objets.

Il faudrait recommencer, n'emporter que le strict nécessaire,

mais qu'est-ce que le nécessaire quand on se sent soi-même
     superflu?

Voilà : on est devenu son propre excédent de bagage.

On voudrait tout refourrer en vrac dans les armoires,

s'asseoir en attendant l'instant qui ne saurait plus tarder,

les pieds dans la paille et la tête environnée de poussière;

voir le vide à travers ces murs qui nous ont si longtemps contenus,

avec les traces pâles des souvenirs, l'empreinte des habitudes.

Mais on tourne en rond et chaque pas résonne comme un coup de
     maillet

parmi les bruits qui montent toujours du jardin et de la rue :

des oiseaux, des appels et même des moteurs familiers,

éclats éparpillés d'une ville qui se détraque

et vont rouler dans l'ombre au-dessous des meubles qui ne
     craquent plus.

Très bien. On va partir maintenant de toute manière.

Personne ne nous attend, personne ne viendra nous chercher,

sauf les trois grands gueulards à harnais de cuir et casquette

qui se fichent éperdument de nos états d'âme et ne songent qu'à
     en finir.

C'est simplement l'heure de partir comme si l'on allait à la Poste

en claquant derrière soi la porte et sans même emporter les clés.

Ce qui restera dans les placards – des chaussettes, des poèmes,

des lettres, des photos – quelqu'un pourra bien s'en charger.

MOVING OUT

There's a lot to do yet. A lot. Too much. There's too much to do.
Three fourths of the bags aren't even packed
and from amid the suitcases' huge open jaws
a sickening disorder of clothes and objects flows back.
One should start all over, take only what one really has to,
but what's there to 'has to' when one feels oneself to be the
    overflow?
There you go: one's become superfluous, one's own excess bags.
One wants to stuff everything in a jumble back in the wardrobes,
sit waiting for the moment sure to come without delay,
one's feet in the straw and head surrounded by dust;
see the emptiness through these walls that so long contained us,
with the pale traces of memories, habit's mark.
But one goes around in circles and each step resonates like a
    mallet's blow
among the sounds still rising from the garden and the street:
birds, cries, even motors with a familiar thrum and pop,
scattered fragments of a city breaking down and weak
and in the shadows underneath rolls furniture whose creaking has
    stopped.
Right. In any case now it'll be time to go.
No one's waiting for us, no one will come pick us up,
except the three big loud lugs with leather harnesses and hats
who couldn't care less how we're feeling and only want to stop.
It's merely time to leave as if heading down to the Post Office
banging the door shut behind oneself without even taking the keys.
What's left in the cupboards – socks, poems, letters, pictures –
someone or other will make sure it's taken away.
And it'll all disappear into big trash bins on wheels,

Et tout ça s'en ira dans les grandes poubelles à roulettes,
puis dans les dépotoirs, aux Puces, chez des soldeurs,
et de là dans d'autres vies où ces choses sans mémoire
seront pourtant les seules à se souvenir de nous.
Des yeux d'enfant écarquillés dans les albums continueront de
    luire,
comme luisent les étoiles mortes et les cassures du charbon.
Et nous qui aurons tant aimé voir passer les nuages,
nous ne durerons plus que dans l'ombre intermittente qu'ils
    jettent au fond
des chambres, et dans les yeux des vivants qui caressent
le temps sur leurs genoux comme un chat endormi.
Nous dévalerons sans fin le long des parois vaporeuses,
sous le poids de ce que nous aurons abandonné.

then garbage dumps, flea markets, cheap five and dimes,
and from there into other lives where these memoryless things
will nonetheless be the only ones to remember us.
Children's wide eyes in albums will continue to shine,
as dead stars and cracks in pieces of coal do.
And we who'll have so liked watching clouds pass,
We'll only last there in the intermittent shadow they throw
within rooms, and into the eyes of the living who caress
time on their knees like a sleeping cat.
We'll hurtle endlessly down along the vaporous inner walls,
under the weight of what we'll have given up.

LES MAINS VIDES

Un grand coup d'accélérateur nous a jetés par-dessus nos vies
et comme des insensés nous avons adoré ce mouvement,
cette ivresse de voir défiler à toute allure visages et campagnes,
ne nous retournant que pour lancer un rire déjà plein d'ombre
à tous ceux que nous dépassions, humbles cantonniers du temps,
penchés dans les fossés entre le ciel et les orties,
mais debout un instant,
soudain droits dans leur étonnement comme des victimes ou
    comme des juges.
Nous ne ralentissions que pour prendre à témoin de notre
    merveilleuse vitesse
la patiente, la nourrice errante, là-haut, avec rien dans les bras,
son vieux dos rond en deuil bravant la foire glaciale des astres,
sa face d'inexpressif amour tendue contre l'os de nos fronts
et berçant machinalement notre orgueil et notre solitude.
Chère vieille Chinoise. Cher vieux chariot.
Chère vieille histoire connue par coeur mais c'est toujours la même
    surprise
quand elle fait brouter cette vache rouge gravide sur l'horizon,
puis élève un bol de lait frais pour désaltérer la folie
ou, dans un train de nuit dont les rideaux battent et claquent
    comme des dents,
pose un doigt transparent sur les yeux que la peur de mourir
    éveille
et qui plongent de nouveau vers des places pensives comme des
    lavoirs,
des pelouses sur lesquelles a déteint l'encre invisible des rêves.
Et toi aussi pourtant nous t'avons laissée derrière nous,
passés de l'autre côté comme des enfants qui, après la lessive,

EMPTY-HANDED

A heavy step on the accelerator threw us headlong over our lives
and as if insane we adored this movement,
this exhilaration of seeing faces and landscapes flash by,
turning around only to let out a laugh already heavy with shadow
at all those we were overtaking, time's humble roadworkers,
bent over in the ditches between the sky and the nettles,
but upright for an instant,
suddenly straight in their astonishment like victims or judges.
We'd only slow down to take as witness of our wonderful speed
the patient one, the wandering nurse, up above, with nothing in her
    arms,
her old grieving round back braving the ice-cold fair of stars,
her side that shows inexpressive love lain against the bone's line of
    our faces
and cradling without thinking our solitude and our pride.
Dear subtle old Chinese woman. Dear old Bear.
Dear old story known by heart but it's always the same surprise
when she makes that red gravid cow on the horizon there graze,
then raises a bowl of fresh milk to quench madness's thirst
or, in a night train whose curtains beat and chatter like teeth,
places a transparent finger on the eyes that the fear of dying wakes
and that plunge again toward pensive places like washtubs,
like lawns onto which the invisible ink of dreams has run.
And yet you too, we left you behind us,
we'd gone to the other side like children who, the washing done,
play in the labyrinths of hanging tablecloths and sheets,
while a prowling evening goes to stretch out on the hill
and the blaze breaks out within the homes' windowpanes.
We weren't wanting to go so far so fast,

jouent dans les labyrinthes des nappes et des draps étendus,
pendant qu'un soir rôdeur va s'allonger sur la colline
et que l'incendie éclate au fond des vitres des maisons.
Nous ne voulions pas aller aussi loin aussi vite,
il aurait fallu prendre le temps.
Mais le temps nous a pris en route comme un camionneur ivre,
hurlant des plaisanteries obscènes pour couvrir le bruit du moteur,
et gaiement et lâchement nous avons approuvé par politesse
jusqu'à ce qu'il freine d'un coup brutal et nous dise : c'est là,
vous y êtes, descendez, j'ai autre chose à faire maintenant.
Et on l'a vu virer avec rage dans la poussière,
repartir dans la direction d'où nous étions venus,
un peu surpris, les bras ballants, osant à peine croire
que la route toujours bondissante dût s'effondrer ici.
Ici, du reste, c'est un endroit tranquille,
sous un haut talus de sable herbeux qui semble cacher la mer
et retenir le temps assoupi comme au fond d'une barque.
Mais aucune rumeur, pas un souffle, plus un oiseau.
Tôt ou tard il faudra gravir quand même pour se rendre compte,
savoir d'où descend cette lumière sans ombre et dont la douceur
    nous saisit
quand nous voyons comme elle éclaire les lointains à présent
    déserts de la route
et le poids incompréhensible du vide entre nos mains.

time should have been taken.
But time took us on its way like a truck driver who's drunk,
howling dirty jokes to drown out the diesel whir,
and we happy cowards approved out of politeness
until suddenly he braked hard and said: there,
you're here now, get out, I've got other things to do.
And we saw him spin around angrily in the dust,
head off again in the direction we'd come from,
a bit surprised, our arms dangling, barely able to believe
the always jumping road had to collapse just here.
Here, moreover, is a peaceful spot,
under a high bank of grassy sand which seems to hide the sea
and hold back dozing time as within the depths of a small boat.
But not a single murmur, or breath, or bird.
Sooner or later one really must climb to comprehend,
to know where this shadowless light flows down from, its
    gentleness seizing us
when we see it illuminate the road's now deserted distances
and the incomprehensible weight of the emptiness between our
    hands.

RETOUR AU CALME

Et cependant là-haut de lents volumineux nuages
Passent, retour de quelle autre vaine moisson,
Souverains sous la charge et déversant à l'horizon
Leur fragile trésor de neige qui s'étage
En montagnes sans poids, en palais changeants où le feu
Du soir couve.

             Or nous fûmes pareils à vous, nuages
Qui vous aventurez dans la flamme du bleu
Et laissez dire au vent qui vous pousse et vous remodèle,
S'il en est un le sens du trajet hasardeux.
Ainsi votre monumentale indolence est fidèle
Au souffle qui toujours vous dissipe en vapeurs,
Et notre destin nuageux lui-même se dévide
Entre les mains du temps innocentes et vides
Après nous avoir bousculés vers l'ombre, par des lueurs.

RETURN TO CALM

And meanwhile up above slow bulky clouds
Pass, the return of some other vain harvest, sovereign
Under the load and pouring out, there on the horizon,
Their fragile treasure of snow that rises in tiers
Of weightless mountains, of shifting palaces where
Evening's fire smolders.
                    In this we resembled you, clouds
That venture into the blue's flame
And let the wind that pushes and remodels you be told
The meaning, if there is one, of the hazardous route.
Thus your monumental laziness is faithful
To the breath that always disperses you in vapors,
And our cloudy fate itself unwinds
Between the innocent empty hands of time
After having moved us sharply toward darkness, by glimmers.

AUX PASSAGÈRES

TO SHORT-LIVED LOVES

LE VISAGE CACHÉ

Ces visages qui tour à tour m'auront brûlé,
Que voilaient-ils, de quelle invisible figure
Étaient-ils le symbole ou le caricature,
Ou bien la vérité changeante et vouée à l'oubli?
Mais quand je les revois, surgis de ces replis
Où la cendre à présent voisine avec la roche,
Ne laissant plus au feu qu'un médiocre aliment,
Je redoute un peu moins l'ombre qui se rapproche
Et le souci du vrai s'endort en moi comme un enfant
Fatigué du voyage.

THE HIDDEN FACE

These faces that by turns will have burnt me,
What veils were they drawing, of what hidden
Figure were they the symbol, the caricature,
Or the truth ever changing, forgotten?
But I see them again, arisen from
These folds where ash and rock are side by side,
Leaving for fire only meager food,
And fear somewhat less darkness as it nears
And concern for truth falls asleep within me like a child
Tired from traveling.

CORRESPONDANCE

Vous m'écrivez. Comme en songe vous m'écrivez.
Pourtant ce n'est plus vous vraiment qui m'écrivez, ni moi
Qui reçois comme en songe votre lettre.
Les nouvelles s'en vont, s'égarent et parviennent
Après un temps si long qu'on ne sait plus à quoi
Font allusion ces mots dont l'encre violente s'efface;
Et qui, sur la photo qui a pâli dans l'enveloppe,
Sourit encore aux soleils disparus.

CORRESPONDENCE

You write me. As if in a dream you write me
Yet it's not really you who writes me, nor me
Who receives as if in a dream your letter.
The news leaves, gets lost and arrives
After such a long time one no longer knows
What these words with their fading violent ink refer to;
And who, in the photo that's gone pale in the envelope,
Still smiles at forgotten suns.

LE BAISER

Bientôt l'épaisse odeur de brioche dans les salons
Mêlée à celle des enfants qui s'échauffent – exquises,
Graves avec leur premier fard, les premiers hauts talons,
La Bohémienne, la Fée et deux ou trois Marquises
(Parmi les Arlequins, Pierrots et Gaulois chevelus,
Je paradais comme de juste en costume de zouave) –
Le soir vint doucement sans qu'on s'en aperçoive :
Quelques lampes roses, Cythère atteinte, et jamais plus.
Très tard, dans la chambre du fond, celle dont le visage
Était l'arc, la flèche et le faon lunaire, consentit
Un seul baiser dans un miroir, ciel de ce travesti
Où mes lèvres n'auront touché que ma glaçante image.

THE KISS

Soon the thick smell of brioche in the main rooms
Mixed with that of children warming up – exquisite, this
Seriousness in their first makeup, their first high heels,
The Bohemian Woman, the Fairy, a few Marchionesses
(Amidst the Harlequins, Pierrots and bearded Gauls,
I strutted about as befits one dressed as a zouave) –
Evening fell gently, hardly perceived:
A few rosy lamps, Cythera reached, and never more.
Quite late, in the farthest-back room, she whose face
Was the moonlike arrow, bow and fawn, granted
A single kiss in a mirror, the sky of this cross-dressed
Boy where my lips touched my own chilling trace.

LE SENTIER

On n'irait pas beaucoup plus loin que le sentier
Qui passait sous les yeux embués des prunelles
Dans l'été lent comme des vêpres solennelles,
À douze ans quand l'amour n'était pas un métier
Dont il faut connaître les règles.
                                On aimait
Comme on respire ou bien déjà comme on s'essouffle,
Car si la suite ne fut pas qu'attirance du soufre
Qui brûle sous le linge et les larmes, jamais,
Vers la marche du ciel qu'on n'aura pas gravie,
De nouveau le sentier et le soir suspendu
Devant cet orme lumineux comme la vie,
Profond comme elle, et depuis longtemps abattu.

(Cependant j'ai revu le sentier, et les haies
Qui le gardent et n'ont pas tellement changé.
Il s'en revint tout droit, fidèle messager
D'autrefois, comme si c'étaient les mêmes baies
Qui, brillant sous la ronce, attendaient mon retour,
Pour me dire : le temps n'est pas chose certaine
Et le soir, tu le vois, demeure la fontaine
Où boire de nouveau le premier lait d'amour.

Mais de longtemps ont défleuri les aubépines.
Qu'aurais-je pu cueillir, ici? Quelques épines,
Ou la mûre tardive au jet d'épais sang noir.
Et si j'avais trouvé des fleurs avec le soir
Immobile un instant dans l'herbe qui détale
Vers l'ombre, il eût fallu les porter sur la dalle
Qui n'enferme plus rien qu'on veuille encore voir.

THE FOOTPATH

We wouldn't go much farther than the footpath
That passed under the plum trees' misty eyes
In the summer slow as evening prayers,
At twelve years old when love wasn't a craft
Whose rules need to be known.
                              We loved
As one breathes or already as running out of breath hurts,
For if what followed was but attraction of the sulphur
That burns under clothes and tears, never,
Toward the step to heaven we won't have climbed,
Again the footpath and the evening suspended
Before this elm luminous as life, to find
It as deep as life, and long since humbled.

(Nonetheless I've seen the footpath again, and the hedges
That keep watch and haven't really shown changes.
It comes back quite straight, a faithful messenger
Of days past, as if it were the same berries
Gleaming under the brambles, awaiting my return as I roved
To say: time is most uncertain
And evening, you well see, remains the fountain
At which to drink again the first milk of love.

But it's ages since the flowers are gone from the hawthorn.
What could I really have gathered, here? A few thorns,
Or the late berry with its jet of blood thick and black.
And if I had found flowers to bring back
With the evening still for an instant in the grass
That speeds toward darkness, I'd have carried them to the slab
That encloses nothing of which one might still keep track.

Dors, là, si c'est dormir, la plus humble espérance;
Dors, petite à jamais pour moi qui n'ai pas su
La vie amère ensuite, et le tendre tissu
De la joue et du coeur gâté pour l'endurance
À vivre comme on boit sans goût, pour oublier.
Et qu'oubli ni sommeil désormais ne consentent
À ton retour en songe, en ombre frémissante
Au-devant de ma main ouverte en ce sentier.)

Sleep, there, if it's sleeping that's the humblest hope;
Sleep, young girl for always to me who didn't know
The bitter life to follow, and the tissue forever
Tender of the cheek and of the heart spoiled to endure
Living like one drinks without taste, to forget at last.
And may neither forgetting nor sleep henceforth consent
To your return in dreams, as a quivering shadow, absent,
To my open outstretched hand here upon this footpath.)

LA FUGITIVE

Jamais je n'ai revu l'irréelle cycliste
Qui surgit un beau jour au milieu de nos jeux
Puis se tint à l'écart, un sourire ombrageux,
Sagace aux lèvres, comme un elfe cabaliste.
Mais lorsque notre ardeur, inquiète, eut décru,
Elle s'évanouit comme elle avait paru
Et je la poursuivis en vain sur ma bécane.
Par tous les chemins bleus il me semble, depuis,
Fille du vent candide et mère de l'arcane,
Que c'est elle encore et toujours que je poursuis.

THE FUGITIVE

Never again did I see the unreal cyclist
Who appeared out of nowhere once during our games
Then kept at a distance, with her nervous smile,
Shrewd round the lips, a sort of cabalist elf.
But when our ardor, worried, had diminished,
As mysteriously as she'd appeared she vanished
And I went after her on my bike in vain.
Along every blue lane since then it seems to me it's her,
Daughter of the open wind and mother of the arcane,
Again and always I'm looking for.

TRISTAN

De la sale mansarde où j'étais le plus jeune
Et l'amour un événement semestriel,
On m'expulsa. Plus tard, exalté par ce jeûne,
Je raccompagnai seul Simone vers Triel.
Sur les coteaux entre la forêt et la Seine,
La lune adoucissait son profil un peu dur
Mais presque virginal malgré l'épreuve obscène
Qu'il venait de subir (car j'écoutais au mur
Tout en lisant les vers de quelque idéaliste).
Et nous flânions par les pentes, main dans la main.
L'occasion d'avoir mon tour en bout de liste
S'est présentée à plus d'un détour du chemin.
Mais "quels salauds, murmurait-elle, j'en ai marre",
Et j'allais comme avec un glaive à son côté.
Le fleuve en bas brillait aussi dans la nuit noire
Et blanche où flotte encore une intacte beauté.

TRISTAN

From the dirty garret I got kicked out at last,
Where but twice yearly was any love felt,
And me the youngest. Later, given wings by this fast,
Quite by myself I accompanied Simone to Triel.
On the hillsides between the forest and the Seine,
The moon softened her profile – slightly tough
But almost virginal despite the ordeal, frankly obscene,
It had just happened to undergo (for I heard rough
Sounds at the wall while reading the verse of some idealist).
And we strolled along the slopes, hand in hand,
The chance to have my turn at the end of the list
Presented itself at more than one turn in the land.
But "what bastards," she murmured, "I'm sick of it,"
And me like a two-edged sword at her side.
The river below glistened as well in the thick of it,
The black and white night where intact beauty still abides.

LES YEUX

Menue et brune, de profil dans l'immense bureau
Retentissant de claviers secs, du strident téléphone :
Je m'attardais là sans prétexte, un vague bordereau
Entre les doigts, jusqu'à ce que la stature bouffonne
Du Chef muet à mon côté m'intime d'en finir.
Alors comme au fond d'un jour terne un rayon soudain cueille
Deux étangs cachés où le ciel tout entier se recueille,
Vite ses yeux m'éblouissaient d'un pur jet de saphir.
Si bien que rappelé toujours au bord de la fontaine,
Je faillis y boire, une nuit tortueuse. Mais coi
Devant son azur assombri – plus proche, plus lointaine –
J'ai fait y flotter pour longtemps le trouble d'un "pourquoi?"

EYES

Slim and dark she stood, in profile in the huge office
Resounding with dry keyboards, with loud phones:
I lingered there without pretext, some invoice
Curled in hand, until the silent boss standing like a buffoon
At my side implied I should give it a rest.
Then as deep within a grey day where a ray suddenly pulls
Into focus two hidden ponds where the whole sky grows full,
Quickly her eyes dazzled me with sapphire, the purest and best.
So much so that, brought back always to the fountain's edge,
I nearly drank, one tortuous night. But I foundered
Speechless before her darkened skies – nearer, farther – where
I let linger a good while a "why?" most troubled.

LA TASSE

Je me souviens du froid, d'une longue avenue
Entre des parcs déserts, et du bourdonnement
De la voix qui disait : "Si vous l'aviez connue
Autrefois... Et pourtant... Mais elle est sûrement
Absente." Et je voyais, entre les fleurs du givre,
Éclore et disparaître un visage trop pur
Sur des pentes de neige ouvertes comme un livre
Où rien n'était encore inscrit de ce futur.
Puis : l'immeuble en cristal dans la chaste lumière,
Et le soupir voluptueux d'un ascenseur;
La clé qui tourne, le silence. Et la première
Chose que j'aperçus, le signe avertisseur,
Fut cette tasse vide au milieu d'une table
Dans la clarté distante et blanche de l'hiver
Où je t'ai reconnu, visage véritable,
Neige de solitude, et ce long regard vert.

THE CUP

I remember the cold, a long avenue
Between empty parks, and the drone
Of the voice that used to say: "If it were you
Who knew her then… And yet… But she's gone,
Surely." And I saw, between frost patterns,
A too-pure face take form and disappear
On banks of snow whose open
Books had nothing yet inscribed of this future.
Then: the crystal building in the chaste light,
And the voluptuous sigh of an elevator;
The key that turns, the silence. And the first
Thing I noticed, the warning sign that made me sure,
Was that empty cup in the middle of a table
In winter's distant white clearness
Where I recognized you, the genuine face,
Snow of solitude, and this long green look.

L'INVISIBLE

Pour des yeux couleur d'eau, j'ai quelque temps hanté
Un superbe entresol situé du côté
Le plus mallarméen du quartier Saint-Lazare.
On m'y jugeait au naturel assez bizarre
Et, j'imagine, pas assez entreprenant.
Mais le moyen, dans un tumulte permanent?
C'était en somme une espèce de phalanstère.
À sa guise on vivait là plus ou moins par terre,
Sans autres meubles que des cendriers, des lits
Défaits, comme agités encore d'un roulis,
Qu'on devinait sous une épaisseur d'ombre morte
Quand cherchant la cuisine on se trompait de porte.
Et toujours quand on en revenait, deux ou trois
Personnages nouveaux faisaient valoir leurs droits
À s'incruster sur votre espace de moquette
Et courtiser à votre place la coquette
Aux yeux d'eau qui, pour mieux me séduire, vantait
Sa compagne de chambre en voyage. C'était
Bien assez de son nom pour y croire. Semaine
Après semaine, je guettai le phénomène
En vain. Si bien que rien n'a jamais démenti
Le charme de ces trois syllabes : Charity.
(En même temps j'aimais Véra, Margot, Rosine;
J'eusse aimé mon voisin s'il eût été voisine
Et, comme je flânais à tire-larigot,
Pour des passantes j'oubliais Véra, Margot,
Rosine, revenant apaiser mes fringales
Imaginaires dans les bornes conjugales,
N'abandonnant cet équilibre de danseur

THE INVISIBLE

For eyes the color of water, for a time I haunted
A superb entresol situated
On the most Mallarmean side of Saint-Lazare.
I was judged there on my admittedly bizarre
Temperament and thought to be, I imagine, lacking drive.
But ambition, in a place so alive
With bustle, in sum a kind of phalanstery?
One did as one pleased, living in community,
Sleeping on the ground, ashtrays the only furniture,
Beds unmade as if stirred by winds in nature,
Guessed at beneath dead shadow – thick, all the more
For having looked for the kitchen and found the wrong door.
And always when one returned, two or three
New characters insisted the others see
Things their way – their right to your patch of carpet
And to court in your place the coquette
With eyes clear like water who, to better seduce me, says
Charming words about her roommate on a trip. It was
Her name that helped me fully believe. Week
After week I kept watch, to seek
Solace. In vain. So much so that nothing belied for me
The charm of those three syllables: Charity.
(At the same time I loved Vera, Margot, Rosine;
I might have loved my neighbor if he were a she
And, since to my heart's content I strolled solo,
For passing women I forgot Vera, Margot,
Rosine, returning to appease my imaginary hunger
Within the limits of the conjugal order,
Abandoning this dancer's balance only

Que pour celle qui fut toujours l'unique soeur
Avec son propre élan vers l'amour invisible.
Et, délivrés, flottant dans un monde paisible,
L'un pour l'autre parfois de nouveau nous étions
L'invisible saisi sans gages ni questions.)

For she who was the one always
True sister with her own surge toward invisible love.
And, delivered, we floated in a peaceful world, of
Being at times for each other again
The invisible seized without wagers or questions.)

TRAVERSÉE DE BOLOGNE

J'aimais la Romaine un peu grasse et qui crânait,
Femme je ne sais plus de quel fameux trombone :
Elle était belle comme un Raphaël et bonne
À peu près comme une harpie. Un vieux carnet
Conserve le croquis maladroit qui la campe
Dans l'escalier où je pouvais un court instant
L'accompagner, fringant comme un jeune hippocampe,
Et l'adorer pour ainsi dire à bout portant.
Mais légère dans son nuage de batistes,
Elle disparassait à l'entrée-des-artistes
Entre deux obsédants accords de Mal Waldron.
Et je me retrouvais pâle sur le goudron,
Heureux pourtant de fuir par la rue en arcades
Vers l'amoureuse obscurité, dans la chaleur,
Quelquefois m'arrêtant, repartant par saccades
Après avoir été, comme un cambrioleur,
Tout au fond d'une cour où, douce comme l'huile,
La lune reluisait sur le bord de la tuile
Et descendait prudente, en marchant de côté,
Jusqu'à la niche où quelque lare délité
Riait de la sentir effleurer sa tunique.
Puis elle saupoudrait de neige carbonique
La ville tour à tour noir d'encre et blanc de chaux,
Et je tombais, muet comme un carme déchaux,
Devant l'espace où les basiliques énormes
Ont l'air – surgis du tuf des Nombres et des Formes –
De fours où cuit le pain âcre des trois Vertus,
Ou d'entrepôts déserts qui sont mon vrai domaine.
Alors oubliant tout (Dieu, la belle Romaine),
Je tournais là longtemps comme un énergumène
Avec l'ombre des tours penchant leurs fronts têtus.

CROSSING BOLOGNA

I loved the Roman one, a little heavy, hardly reserved,
The wife of I don't know which famous trombonist:
She was pretty as a Raphaël and kind in all this
About like a Harpy. An old notebook preserves
The clumsy sketch that portrays her – us –
On the stairs where for a flash I felt dashing,
Able to accompany her, a young hippocampus,
Where, so to speak, up tip close I stayed, adoring.
But light in her cloud of batistes,
She disappeared at the entry sign "Artists"
Between two Mal Waldron chords' haunting beat
And I found myself pale on the street,
Happy nonetheless through archway streets to flee
Toward the loving obscurity, in the heat,
Sometimes stopping, starting again with jerky glee
After having been, like a thief,
At the far end of a courtyard where, soft as oil,
The moon gleamed at the edge of the tile
And went down, prudent, walking sideways,
As far as the niche where some crumbling deity
Laughed at the warm glow grazing his tunic.
Then the moon peppered artificial snow, a tonic,
On the town by turns ink black and lime white,
And I fell, mute as a Discalced Carmelite,
Before the space where huge basilicas loom
And seem – surged forth from the tuff of Number and Form –
Like ovens where the three Virtues cook acrid bread, or places
Vast like deserted entrepôts, my true domain.
And so forgetting everything (God, the pretty Roman one),
I turned there for some time as if crazy or undone
With the towers' shadows leaning in their stubborn faces.

EN FIN DE CONTE
Pour N.

Dans la chambre du fond dorment les amoureuses.
Leurs doigts ont la couleur pensive de l'oubli.
Par la fenêtre ouverte aux campagnes ombreuses
Veille un ciel qu'une lune invisible remplit.
Et, comme un fil qu'on a détaché d'une robe,
Une route sinue et brille entre les sourds
Bois de part et d'autre massés qui s'interrogent,
Ne voyant rien venir. Elles dorment toujours.
Et le paysage est le même dans leur rêve :
Une chambre perdue au fond d'une maison
Qui n'existe plus, dont la fenêtre s'élève
Comme un doigt sur la lèvre en feu de l'horizon.

Mais celle qui dormait comme les orphelines,
Seule au fond des couloirs craquants d'un vieux château,
La lune, se glissant derrière les collines,
Chaque nuit pénétrait ses rêves. Et bientôt,
Sans laisser dans son lit la plus légère empreinte,
Elle devint le songe ambulant de la nuit
Qui s'éclairait et dénouait le labyrinthe
De ces chemins au bout desquels le grand jour luit
Sur une ville dont le coeur est l'étendue
De plus en plus profonde à mesure qu'on va.
Et j'avançais de mon côté, de rue en rue —
Ainsi ce qui devait arriver arriva.

AT TALE'S END
For N.

In the end room sleep the lovers.
Their fingers have the pensive color of forgetting.
At the window open to the countryside shadows
A sky keeps watch that an invisible moon keeps filling.
And, like a thread one has removed from a dress,
A road winds and glistens between the still
Woods here and there massed that question
Themselves, seeing nothing coming. They sleep still.
And the landscape's the same in their dream:
A lost room within a house
That no longer exists, whose window rises as if between
House and sky, a finger on the horizon's burning lip.

But she who slept like the orphans,
Alone at the end of an old castle's brittle halls,
The moon, sliding itself behind the hills,
Each night entered her dreams. And soon,
Without leaving in her bed the slightest imprint,
She became the night's itinerant dream
That lit up and untangled the labyrinth
Of these paths at whose end the daylight gleams
On a town whose heart is the expanse
That grows increasingly deep the farther one goes.
And I went my way from street to street, advanced —
What was to happen did — and so the tale closes.

NOUVELLES IMPRESSIONS FERROVIAIRES

NEW RAILWAY IMPRESSIONS

L'AUTORAIL

En hiver, à midi, quand le soleil chauffe déjà,
On peut ouvrir en grand la fenêtre de la cuisine,
Et des sons indolents descendent jusqu'en bas
Du village, comme en été, vers la ligne du bois,
Ces cloches au battant d'eau claire ou de lait froid
Qui désaltéraient la vallée et la bête assoupie
Ronflant dans les fourrés comme une impossible toupie.
Sur deux notes (*oui, non, oui, non,* ou bien *pour-quoi*),
L'autorail corne encore à deux heures : on voit
Entre les saules blondissant déjà sur la rivière
Les yeux des étés disparus briller à la portière.

THE RAILCAR

In winter, at noon, with the sun already getting warm,
You can open wide the kitchen window,
And languid sounds drift all the way down
To the village, as in summer, near the woods below,
These bells with their clappers' clear water or cold milk show
That soothed the valley and the animal sleeping lazily,
Snoring in the underbrush like a top spinning impossibly.
On two notes (*yes, no,* or *why-then, yes, no*),
The train sounds again at two: and so
It is you see between willows turning gold already on the river
The eyes of bygone summers glitter at the railcar door.

REMBLAIS

La rose nocturne se rouvre et dévore Longwy:
Le dieu du fer y hurle et s'abîme dans la coulée
Pour devenir ces longs rails froids où s'échappe ma vie
En tournant sans cesse, en tournant,
Cherchant le feu d'où monte avec indolence en fumée
Tout ce que j'ai fauché de fleurs sur les remblais du temps.
Un sentier bronche et tousse au fond des forêts endormies;
Les clairières près des étangs referment leur manteau.
Dans un pré, le soleil, brillant comme un vieux meuble, éclaire
Broutant, le cou tendu sur l'herbe tutélaire,
Quatre petits chevaux.

EMBANKMENTS

The night rose reopens and swallows up Longwy:
There the god of iron howls and founders in the castings
To become these long cold rails where my life slips away
Turning without end, turning,
Looking for the fire from which rises with smoky
Languor the flowers reaped on time's embankments. Sleeping
Forests reveal a footpath that stumbles, coughs; the glades
Near the ponds close back up their coat.
In a meadow, the sun, with the gleam of old furniture, lights
Up, grazing, necks held out over the tutelary grass,
Four small colts.

C F F

Ces wagons fédéraux feutrés passent, entre Dijon
Et Montbard, un massif couvert d'épaisse forêt celte
Où viennent rôder les troupeaux nuageux du Morvan.
Alors aux coteaux de cassis et de raisin succèdent
Des défilés où le brouillard s'enfonce en titubant.
Puis le soleil tombé comme un seau dans un puits, éclaire
Des près en pente où j'ai dû vivre innocent autrefois.
Un peu plus tard, des deux côtés du canal de Bourgogne,
Tout embuée d'or la campagne a dit : Je me souviens,
Redépliant une étendue ancienne où l'on n'aborde
Jamais (et pourtant je m'enfuis sous les rayons du soir
Par des tas de charbon, des fossés qui gardent la trace
D'existences mauvaises dont je ne sais presque rien,
Sinon qu'elles pourraient voler jusqu'à mon apparence
Pour n'en laisser que ce reflet qui flotte en transparence
Sur l'horizon plus sombre, et déroute le contrôleur).

SWISS FEDERAL RAIL

These smooth Swiss federal railcars pass, between Dijon
And Montbard, a massif covered with thick celtic forest
Where the Morvan's cloudy flocks come to roam.
Then the slopes of blackcurrants and grapes give way
To narrow passes where the mist unsteadily plunges.
Next the sun fallen like a bucket in a well lights
The sloping meadows where I doubtless lived innocent in days
    past.
A bit later, from both sides of the Bourgogne canal,
All misted in gold the countryside said: I recall,
Unfolding anew an age-old expanse where one never
Lands (and yet I run away under the evening rays
Along piles of coal, ditches that retain the trace
Of unpleasant lives of which I know almost nothing at all,
Except that they could fly here to my aspect
To leave only what floats clear, transparent, reflects
On the darker horizon and diverts the conductor).

VAGUE WAGON

En s'éveillant le cou cassé contre la vitre
Où frénétiquement l'os bien plat de son front
Vibre, la part enténébrée et vide de ma personne
Aperçoit des bois noirs et si noirs en couronne qu'ils sont
Sur le point de se résorber dans l'indiscontinue
Fureur d'un contre-jour d'orage un peu trop blanc.
Puis on dirait que ce paysage éternue
Et m'expulse d'un songe ou du tiède néant.
C'est un début d'après-midi, l'heure sournoise
Qui vous guette d'un oeil pâle dans les sentiers:
Au bout de chaque feuille, une goutte d'eau froide
Tremble, et ronde elle vous enferme avec le monde entier.
Cependant je suis sûr de n'avoir jamais vu ce site,
Comme il est évident aussi qu'il m'en souvient.
D'autres demi-dormeurs autour de moi s'agitent
Parmi des souvenirs qui ressemblent peut-être aux miens.
Mais le paysage, ou le rêve, encore une fois change,
Et le train file avec ce poids aérien
De mémoires et de sommeils qui se mélangent.

HAZY ROAMING CAR

Awaking with my neck bent against the window
Where the quite flat face bone vibrates, frenzied,
The empty, shadowy part of me
Sees black woods and so black like wreaths
As to be on the verge of resorption in the indiscontinuous
Furor of a too-white backlit storm. Then you might say
With its breath this landscape sneezes
And expels me from tepid nothingness, from a daydream.
It's early afternoon, the sly hour
That tracks you with its pale eye in the footpaths:
At the end of each leaf, a cold drop of water
Trembles, and round it surrounds you with the whole world held
    fast.
Nonetheless I'm sure I never saw this site,
Just as it's obvious I recall it.
Other half-sleepers around me stir
Amid remembrances perhaps like mine, like this.
But the landscape, or the dream, changes yet again,
And the train flies on with this ethereal weight
Of memories and sleeps intermingling.

LE TUNNEL DE SAINCAIZE

L'herbe envahit avant la gare de Saincaize
La voie à l'abandon qui va, par un tunnel
Couronné de cytise et plein d'ombre mauvaise,
Rejoindre cette halte où le soir éternel
Attend le long du quai, pour la correspondance,
Le voyageur que l'âge a fait théologien
Ou sceptique. Soumis à la molle cadence,
Il s'endort. Et déjà voici Briare, Gien,
Et la Loire qui se prélasse entre des sables
Sur le miroitement de ses fins bracelets.
Trop tard alors pour les courbes insaisissables
Que prolongent pourtant des chemins violets,
Sous les feuilles, comme les yeux de Perséphone,
Et qu'on aurait suivis dans l'ombre sans faux pas.
Mais en rêve peut-être... Et, comme au téléphone,
On s'éveille en criant : ne cou, ne coupez pas.

THE SAINCAIZE TUNNEL

The grass overruns before the station "Saincaize"
The neglected line that goes, via a tunnel
Crowned with laburnum and full of unpleasant darkness,
To join this stop where the evening, eternal,
Awaits along the platform, for a connection,
The traveler whom age has made a theologian
Or a skeptic. Subjugated to the soft rhythm,
He sleeps. And already there's Briare, Gien,
And the Loire that basks between the sands
In the shimmer of its fine bracelets.
Too late then for the elusive curves
Nonetheless prolonged by violet paths,
Under the leaves, like the eyes of Persephone,
With which in the darkness one could easily have kept up.
But in a dream perhaps... And, as on the phone,
One awakes, crying out: don't ha, don't hang up.

SOLEIL SAUTEUR

Entre les nappes de brouillard, des bois bondissent
Et soufflent à travers leur poil hérissé roux,
Comme des sangliers crevant ronces et houx
Pour rôder autour des villages qui pâlissent.
En même temps le ciel se déchire : du bleu
En flaque ardente, où s'est creusé le pas d'un ange,
Fulgure et tout autour dévore les nuages,
Puis tout s'enveloppe à nouveau de brume : il pleut
Horizontalement en versets sur les vitres
Où l'on voit le visage en détresse de tous
Les voyageurs flotter, secoués par la toux
Caverneuse des ponts quand, de plus en plus vite,
Luit, s'éteint de nouveau le disque d'étain froid
Qui resurgit de la vapeur et de la suie,
Tendu comme un miroir embué qui s'essuie
À la brosse hirsute et fumeuse des bois.
Et comme sans arrêt, à la même cadence,
On tourne à travers ces massifs inconsistants,
À gauche, à droite, à gauche, on dirait par instants
Que le soleil combat avec lui-même, ou danse.

JUMPING SUN

Among the patches of fog, woods leap
And puff through their red bristled hair,
As when brambles and holly are trampled by boar
Roaming around villages that grow pale and weak.
At the same time the sky tears:
Blue in fiery pools, with angel-step holes,
Across the whole periphery consumes the clouds,
Then the whole is enveloped again in haze:
Horizontal verses of rain on the windowpanes
Where you see every traveler's distressed face
Float, shaken by the cavernous
Cough of bridges when the sun's disk quickens –
Cold as tin shines and is snuffed
And resurfaces from under soot and vapor,
Held out like a misted-over mirror
Drying itself with the woods' hirsute, smoky brush.
And, as if endlessly, at the same cadence,
We turn through these colorless mountains,
Left, right, left, here and there you could say
The sun fights itself, or dances.

TRIAGES

Des bois exubérants poussent dans les usines
Au bord d'un fleuve frais comme du marbre d'eau.
Près des pontons on voit de sveltes sarrasines
Qui plongent de profil et remontent de dos
Sur le rivage où leur corps brille comme l'huile.
La brique, le ciment, les ardoises, la tuile
Se calcinent par les triages sans couleur
Où des wagons bondés tirent dans leurs étuves
Une foule muette. Et la pâle chaleur
Enfume tout le ciel comme plusieurs Vésuves.
Les routes ne sont plus que cendre de papier
Qui se recroqueville. Un soleil estropié,
Fuyant sa propre odeur de poil et de soudure,
Boitille comme un chien âgé de pont en pont.
Parfois il disparaît derrière la verdure.
Son reflet qui se noie appelle : il ne répond
Jamais. Seuls les convois dans tous les sens aboient
Le long de l'eau muette où les plongeurs flamboient.

SORTING ZONES

Exuberant woods grow in the factories
Along a river clear as watered marble.
Near the pontoons one sees svelte Saracen girls
Who dive in profile and resurface turned back
On the bank where their collective body gleams like oil.
Brick, cement, slate and tile
Bake along the colorless sorting zones
Where overfull cars tow as if in incubators
A mute crowd. And the pale heat fills
With smoke the whole sky, Vesuvius several times over.
The roads are now only ash of paper
That curls up. A sun disabled,
Fleeing its own smell of hair and solder,
Limps like an aging dog from one bridge to another.
At times it disappears behind the verdure.
Its drowning reflection calls: it never
Answers. Only the convoys all about bark
Over the mute water where divers' flames spark.

CHEZ LEROY

Quand on passe avec l'autorail et qu'on tourne la tête
Vers la colline où l'on voudrait monter une autre fois,
On croit que le chemin qui va du canal chez Leroy
Ménage un raccourci pour atteindre aisément la crête
Et voir l'horizon déroulé comme une autre planète
Jusqu'aux volcans bleus par-dessus les fleuves et les bois.
Or ce chemin qui part résolument, bientôt s'arrête
Dans une cour de ferme en paille et merde et tas de bois
Écroulés près du hangar vide, à part la camionnette
Sans portière (pour les poulets) et la niche des chiens
Hagards contre un ciel dévoré qui fait cligner la femme
Au tablier mauve, essuyant son front et puis ses mains
Comme toujours. Et le chemin se perd entre des rames
À haricots et le compost qui bouillotte à feu doux
Sous le brasillement funèbre de sa bâche – d'où
(Comme aux creux que le soleil fouille et que le vent déprave)
La puanteur vient sur une aile étrangement suave
Effleurer qui s'attarde au bord de la cour à Leroy.
Il cherche à voir si le chemin ensuite continue
Au-delà de la corde à linge où l'ombre saugrenue
Des rames tarabuste un peu de linge en désarroi
Soulevé dans un geste équivoque de bienvenue.
Mais tout est clos. La femme aboie et les chiens vous conspuent,
Et l'autorail n'est plus qu'un lourd cognement qui décroit.

BY LEROY'S PLACE

When you pass by rail and turn your head
Toward the hill you'd like to climb once more,
You feel sure the path from the canal by Leroy's place
Makes for a shortcut to easily reach the crest
And see the horizon uncoiled like another planet
Up to the blue volcanos above the rivers and woods.
Yet this path that sets off firmly soon stops
In a farmyard filled with straw, shit, piles of wood
Collapsed near the empty barn, except for the doorless
Van (for the chickens) and the haggard dogs'
Kennel against a consumed sky as the mauve-smocked
Woman blinks, wiping as always her face
Then her hands. And the path loses its way between poles
Of beans and the bubbling simmering compost
Under its cover's funereal glow – and oh
(As at the hollow searched by sun, depraved by wind)
The stench that comes on a strangely suave wing
To lightly touch whoever lingers by Leroy's yard.
The visitor looks to see if the path then goes on
Beyond the clothesline where the shadow most odd
Of the rows badgers a bit of laundry not how it should
Be raised in an equivocal gesture of welcome.
But everything's closed. The woman barks, the dogs frown,
The rail's now a heavy banging slowly dead.

TRAVERSÉE DU MORVAN

Deux moutons qui déjà ressemblent à de grosses pelotes de laine
sont plantés au milieu d'un petit pont de pierre pour réfléchir.
D'autres au fond du pré vont broutant avec la certitude
d'accomplir à la perfection tout ce qui leur est prescrit.
On pourrait presque en dire autant du noir motocycliste
qui tient tête un moment au train et ne fait plus qu'un seul bloc
avec sa machine bien huilée qu'on n'entend pas. La route,
brusquement abolie comme la montagne par un talus,
reparaît vide au long des bois d'un brun sourd de ferraille
où d'un trait rapide à la craie se dénombrent les bouleaux.
Il pleut comme il pleut quand on se tient dans une maison fermée,
et toutes ces haies dessinent d'ailleurs une grande maison sans toit
dont la seule habitante profondément préoccupée
est la pluie qui circule d'une pièce à l'autre, changeant
sans y penser la place à jamais fixée d'un village
et son église qui doit sonner les douze coups détrempés de midi.
Puis elle secoue ses doigts de laveuse dans l'eau plate d'une mare
et s'éloigne en les essuyant à son large tablier.
Tout au fond les monts restent couchés comme dans la chambre
    obscure
les aïeux qui ruminent et toussent et râlent sous l'édredon.
Quand le soleil reparaît à l'heure de la sortie de l'école,
comme un pâle vieux sourire aussi derrière d'épais rideaux,
c'est par bonté pour les enfants qui rentrent solitaires vers les
    fermes
par des sentiers sans fleurs qui partout plus tard les suivront.

CROSSING THE MORVAN

Two sheep that already resemble huge balls of wool
are planted in the middle of a small stone bridge to reflect.
Others at the meadow's end go grazing with the certainty
of accomplishing to perfection all they're meant to.
You could almost say as much of the black motorcyclist
keeping up for a moment with the train and who's become
with his well-oiled soundless bike one solid block of machine.
The road, like the mountain abruptly abolished by a bank,
reappears empty along muted scrap-heap brown woods
where one quick chalk stroke draws a count for the silver birch.
It rains as it rains when one keeps still in a closed house,
and all these hedges draw moreover a large house with no roof
whose only deeply preoccupied inhabitant
is the rain, she who goes around from room to room, changing
without thinking a village's forever fixed place
and its church obliged to ring out the twelve wet strokes of
        noon.
Then she shakes her washer's fingers in a pool's still water
and moves away wiping them on her large smock.
Far back the mountains stay lying down as in the dark room
the forebears who brood and cough and grouse under the
        eiderdown.
When the sun reappears at the time school lets out,
like a pale old smile as well behind thick curtains,
it's out of kindness for the children who return alone toward the
        farms
by flowerless footpaths that everywhere later will follow them.

MAUVAISE LUMIÈRE

D'un bout à l'autre de l'horizon qui tourne avec le train,
dans l'eau soupçonneuse des étangs, sous la verrière des gares,
une lumière mal levée, qui ne veut décidément de rien,
erre et flotte en blanc cru dans les effondrements de nuages
puis se ravise et recommence plus pâle un peu plus loin
avec un lourd effort comme pour déterrer une betterave.
L'hésitation s'en va d'arbre en arbre le long des chemins,
passe de biais où des poteaux penchent avec leurs fils qui lâchent
en tirant tout le poids d'un village que l'habitude retient
mais qu'on sent prêt à déserter au trouble de ses lucarnes.
C'est un jour à ne pas dépasser la clôture des jardins,
là où l'herbe est plus haute, les branches plus tordues et plus
    basses,
les souvenirs encore plus perdus, à la recherche d'un coin
pour se défendre, comme au fond d'une incertaine mémoire,
de cette lumière qui ne se rappelle décidément plus rien,
éteinte sous l'oeil fixe des signaux et des premières étoiles.

BAD LIGHT

From one end to the other of the horizon that turns
with the train, in ponds' suspicious water under the stations' glass,
a poorly raised light that indeed wants nothing wanders and floats
harsh white in crumblings of clouds, then
changes its mind and, paler, a bit further off, starts
again with a heavy effort as if to pull up a beet.
Hesitation heads off from tree to tree along the paths,
passes diagonally where poles lean with their wires that let
go taking the whole weight of a village that habit holds
back but that one feels ready to run off seeing its windows fret.
It's a day for not going beyond garden walls,
there where the grass is higher, the branches more twisted and low,
the remembrances still more lost, as each one seeks
a corner for self-defense, as if deep in an uncertain memory,
against this light that indeed recalls nothing,
gone out under the fixed eye of the signals and first stars.

LIGNE DIRECTE

Le soleil n'est ni d'un côté ni de l'autre : midi.
Mais il n'est pas non plus debout au-dessus de ma tête :
À sa propre chaleur il a complètement fondu,
Aspergeant la campagne entre de lourds clochers qui tintent
Et les toits des hangars de tôle en train de prendre feu.
Pas un arbre. La route est un jet d'acier sans défaut.
Ruisselant sous cette cascade épaisse de lumière,
J'ai donc monté jusqu'au repli sombre d'une lisière.
Mais le fil d'ombre où j'espérais laver mes yeux bouillis
N'est encore que du soleil vautré dans le taillis.
Plein de fortes odeurs, de mouches comme un homme sale
Et barbu parmi les débris ménagers qu'il trimbale,
Il croque hébété les cailloux lâchés par un talus.
Au sommet, un train de soleil halète sur la voie
Qui, dans les bois, des deux côtés, aussi loin que l'on voie,
D'un seul jet s'enfonce en tremblant vers des pays perdus.

DIRECT LINE

The sun isn't on one side or the other: noon.
But it also isn't standing above my head:
It's completely melted at its own heat,
Splashing the countryside between bells that ring, heavy,
And the sheet-metal warehouse roofs catching fire, streaked.
Not a tree in sight. The road's a faultless run of steel.
Streaming warmth beneath this light's thick cascade,
I took to climbing to a wood's edge and the dark bend it made,
But the thread of shadow where I hoped to wash my boiled eyes
Is still only sun sprawled in the copse.
Full of bad smells of flies like some dirty bearded man
Amid the household debris lugged along as best he can,
The dazed sun bites into the embankment's loose rocks.
Up top, a train of sun puffs and pants on the track
Which, in the woods, on both sides, all the way back,
At one go plunges trembling toward places lost.

CHEMINS PERDUS

Pareil aux inquiets, aux longs velléitaires
Qui n'auront jamais su choisir un seul chemin,
Tous ceux que j'aperçois, lorsque je passe en train,
Filer à travers bois, dans l'épaisseur des terres,
Me paraissent chacun devenir, tour à tour,
Celui que j'aurais dû suivre sans aucun doute.
Je me dis : la voici, c'est elle, c'est la route
Certaine qu'il faudra revenir prendre un jour.
Mais aussitôt après, sous la viorne et la ronce,
Un sentier couleur d'os ou d'orange prononce
Sa courbe séduisante au détour d'un bosquet,
Et c'est encore un des chemins qui me manquaient.
Puis le bord d'un canal donne une autre réponse
À ce perpétuel élan vers le départ.
Mais je vous aime ainsi, chemins, déserts et libres.
Et tandis que les rails me tiennent à l'écart,
Vous venez vous confondre au réseau de mes fibres.

LOST PATHS

Like those who worry, who never could stand
To decide and never will choose a single path,
All those I notice, as by train I pass,
And see running through woods, in the thickness of lands,
Seem to become, each in turn, my fate,
The one without the slightest doubt I should have followed.
I tell myself: there, that's it, the road
To definitively come back some day and take.
But just as soon after, under the viburnum and brambles,
A bone- or orange-colored footpath utters
Its seductive curve at the turn of a copse
And it's another of the paths I'd long lost.
Then the edge of a canal approaches and offers
A different answer to this endless surge toward departure.
But I love you thus, paths, deserted and free.
And while the rails keep me away, set apart,
You merge with my network of fibers, with me.

TRAIN DE NUIT

Quand un convoi s'arrête aux abords d'un village
En pleine nuit, d'abord le silence l'étreint.
L'espace est comme un mur derrière le vitrage
Qui ne reflète rien que le couloir du train
Et creuse à l'infini la fictive étendue
D'autres couloirs où rôde un même voyageur :
Il voit, mal éveillé, sa figure perdue
Et captive à la fois qui l'imite. Songeur
Encore, il pourrait croire appartenir lui-même
À l'un de ces miroirs innombrables tirant
Du jeu de leurs reflets un parfait stratagème
Pour l'égarer dans un dédale transparent.
Mais pour peu que l'arrêt imprévu se prolonge,
Il entend le mirage où la nuit l'a bouclé
Se remplir de sons crus et creux qui le replongent
Dans un autre univers dont il n'a pas la clé :

Ce sont des chiens. Des chiens. Et quand les chiens s'y mettent
Ne voyant plus la lune en marche au-dessus d'eux,
Mais la pâle phosphorescence d'allumette
Que font sur l'horizon les signaux hasardeux,
On glisse alors au fond d'un autre labyrinthe
Sans issue et sans murs, miroirs ni corridor,
Où chaque nouveau pas vient effacer l'empreinte
Du précédent, et l'on s'enfonce comme on dort.
Des chemins qui montaient descendent. Les prairies
Et les maisons, comme des cartes à jouer,
Tournent entre des doigts savants en jongleries
Rebobinant le fil des heures dénoué.

NIGHT TRAIN

When a train stops at night on the outskirts
Of town, first the silence takes it in its arms, in its hands.
Space is like a wall behind the glass
Which reflects only the train's hall and
Endlessly deepens the imaginary expanse
Of other halls where a similar roaming traveler lives:
Hardly awake he sees how his face haunts,
Imitates him, at once captive and lost. Pensive
Again, he could believe as well it seems
He belongs to one of the countless mirrors that derive
From the play of their reflections a perfect means
To lead him astray in a transparent maze.
But as the unexpected stop extends
Itself, he hears the mirage in which the night sees
Fit to tie him fill with harsh empty sounds that send
Him again to another universe for which he hasn't got the key:

It's dogs. Dogs. And when the dogs howl, bellow,
Seeing no longer the advancing moon
Above but rather a pale match-like glow
From the horizon's rash signals that loom,
One slides then within another labyrinth
Without walls, mirrors, corridors, a dead end one can't leave,
Where each new step erases the print
Of that before, and one sinks deep as when one sleeps.
Paths that went up go down. The grasslands
And the homes, like so many playing cards,
Turn in a kind of juggling act, in learned hands
Rewinding the undone, the hours' thread.

Le monde est à l'envers, et c'est la nuit interne
Qui s'étend alentour alors que le dedans
Se balance et fuit comme une sourde lanterne
Qu'un chien noir et muet tiendrait entre ses dents.

La lune cependant roule d'une colline
À l'autre. On ne voit que l'écume des chevaux
Qui font ainsi bondir cette ronde berline
Dont la lueur répand de grands champs de pavots.
Et les arbres, le vent, les eaux, sur les ficelles
Qu'on tend dans les jardins, un lumineux drap blanc,
Les chemins des forêts et jusqu'aux étincelles
Qui brillent sur les rails, dorment, se dédoublant
Dans leurs rêves hantés par la même lumière
Où des morts frissonnants au bord de leurs tombeaux
Vont révéler par une phrase coutumière
Un secret qui s'en va tout de suite en lambeaux.
Seuls veillent les abois des chiens que met en rage
Le silence qui suit le grincement des freins,
Quand restent en arrêt, la nuit, près d'un village
Dont on ne connaîtra jamais le nom, les trains.

The world is upside down, it's inner night
That spreads itself out while the inside
Sways and flees like a subdued lantern
A dark mute dog might take in its teeth to hold.

The moon nonetheless rolls from one hill
To the next. One sees only the lather of horses
That thus pull in bounds this round berlin
Whose glow scatters great fields of poppies.
And the trees, the wind, the water, on the strings
One hangs in gardens, a luminous white sheet,
The forest paths and even the sparks
That shine on the rails, sleep, opening out
Doubled in their dreams haunted by the same light
Where trembling dead people at the edge of their tombs
Will reveal by a habitual phrase a secret
That quickly falls to bits.
Only the dogs' barks stay watchful, as silence brings
Rage after the squealing of brakes,
When they stay stopped, at night, near a town
Whose name one will never know, the trains.

GRAND TRAIN DE VENT

Il vient un vent plein de terre mouillée,
Plein d'herbe, plein d'ombre de chemins creux,
Un gros vent mou qui sent la nuit rouillée
Près des passages à niveau sans feux.

Il a foncé par les fourrés d'épines
Et bousculé la bordure des bois,
L'eau des étangs, le sommet des collines,
Les jardins fous et les ponts trop étroits.

De tout son poids répandu sur la terre,
Il roule, empoigne et lâche, ressaisit,
La bouche grande ouverte, la paupière
Vague battant sur un oeil obscurci.

Peut-être autour voit-il briller encore,
Dans un rayon qu'il arrache au hasard,
Une fenêtre ou, sous leur toit sonore,
Des fers dressés dans le fond d'un hangar.

Mais tout entier soumis à son tumulte,
Il passe et ramassé sur soi bondit.
Sa masse humide et mugissante exulte
À travers la forêt qui l'applaudit,

Puis va rouvrir, dans le secret des têtes
Qu'elle empêche de craindre et de dormir,
L'espace heureux où divaguent les bêtes
Comme elle sans destin ni souvenir.

BIG TRAIN OF WIND

A wind full of wet earth arrives,
Full of grass, full of hollowed paths' shadow,
A thick muffled wind that smells of rusted night
Near the leveled passages where no lights show.

It tore in by the thicket thorns
And shook the woods' edge,
The pond water, the tops of hills,
The crazed gardens and the too-narrow bridges.

With all its weight scattered over the earth,
It rolls, grabs, lets go, seizes again,
Its hazy eyelids over a wide-open mouth
Lashing an eye grown dim.

Perhaps around it sees shining again,
In a ray torn from chance,
A window or, under their roof that resounds,
Girders set deep in a warehouse's space.

But altogether subjected to its tumult,
It goes past and gathered in itself bounds.
Its howling humid mass exults
Across the forest which applauds,

Then goes to open again, in the secrecy of heads
Whose fear and sleep it prevents,
The happy space where in a haze animals wander,
Like it without fate or remembrance.

L'AIR LIBRE

THE OPEN AIR

QUATRE MARINES

I

La tempête a chargé toute la nuit. Quand on se lève,
Au bas du ciel en madriers l'horizon s'est fendu.
Et la face nocturne invincible fléchit : c'est l'aube
Qui s'infiltre sous les berceaux d'herbe, dans les ravins
Et, le temps d'un éclair, repose au coeur de la rosée.
Un caillou s'enhardit, le bois blotti qui se contient
Fait un pas décisif au bord de la falaise, et la
Proue éblouie entre en tonnant dans la pure vitesse.

II

L'herbe et les pins ne luiraient pas autant sous la lumière
Si le vent n'empoignait chaque touffe pour la polir.
Et pas l'ombre d'une vapeur sur les parois de verre
Qui renferment l'espace et qu'on voit sans arrêt frémir.
Au bout de la route, une dune et l'asphalte crépitent.
L'océan gesticule au bord blanc d'usure du ciel
Qui reflète comme un miroir sphérique le soleil
Pris dans le toit éblouissant de la station-service.
Sur le jetée où rééclate en tonnerre le vent,
Plus fort que cet ébranlement, tandis que l'on avance,
On sent affleurer un massif de calme et de silence
Malgré le continu grelot d'alarme des haubans.

FOUR SEASCAPES

I

The storm charged all night. In waking you see
A split horizon underneath a sky of beams.
And the invincible nocturnal side yields: it's the dawn
Filtering through under the grass arches, in the ravines
And, in a flash, resting cradled at the heart of the dew.
A stone grows bold, the huddled-up wood despite its reserve
Takes a decisive step at the cliff's edge, and the
Dazzled prow enters thunderously into pure speed.

II

The grass and the pines wouldn't shine so under the light
If the wind didn't grab each tuft to polish it.
There's not the shadow of a vapor on the glass walls that
Contain space and keep trembling. If you squint
You see and hear further off the dune's and the asphalt's dry
        agitation.
The ocean gesticulates at the edge of the sky that's white and worn
And that reflects like a spherical mirror the sun
Caught in the dazzling roof of the service station.
On the jetty where the wind bursts again into thunder,
Louder than this shaking, as you advance,
A massif of calm and silence rises to the surface
Despite the shroud lines' continual bells of alarm.

III

Ces jours échoués dans la vase et sans un souffle
Où le temps passe avec le sable qui l'étouffe
Et le cri de la sterne obtuse qui tourne en rond,
Tôt ou tard pourtant je ne sais quelle consolation
Descend du ciel encore indécis qui s'éclaire
Par des chenaux entre des îles de poussière
Vite comblés par des lilas flottant à l'horizon.
Je consens. Je consens à ce glissement de rivière
Vers les sources d'en haut prises dans les deltas
De nuages (le soir immobile sur l'estuaire
S'allonge enfin comme une barque entre mes bras).

IV

Ce que nous voulions nous échoit avec l'heure tardive
Et bien peu de soleil encore (mais il viendra) :
La plage entièrement déserte et de ce beige intact
Et, cousus par un fil de cristal incessant qui se brise,
La vaste dalle de bitume et le ciel en charbon.
Alors pour la première fois de nouveau nous voyons
Le monde horizontal et froid qui pourtant nous protège
Et ne sait pas qu'il est le nôtre et qu'il est beau.

III

These days sunk in the mud and without the slightest breath
Where time goes by with the sand, smothered,
With the dull-witted tern's cry, his pointless turning,
Sooner or later I don't know what consoling something
Comes down somehow from the still undecided sky
Grown clear through channels between dust isles
Quickly filled by lilacs on the horizon, floating.
I accept. I accept this slide so like a river
Toward the sources up above caught there in the clouds
Grouped in deltas (the motionless evening on the estuary
Stretches out at last like a boat between my arms).

IV

What we wanted falls to us as it grows late
And with still very little sun (but it will appear):
The beach entirely deserted and its beige intact
And, sewn by a continual crystal thread that breaks,
The vast slab of asphalt and the charcoal sky.
Then for the first time over again we see
The cold, horizontal world that protects us even so
And doesn't know it's ours and beautiful.

IMAGES D'UN PLATEAU

JANVIER

Le gel sur le chemin de crête a figé dans la boue
Le sillage des tombereaux qui ne rouleront plus.
Et par l'inclinaison heureuse du plateau s'ébrouent
Les fantômes des lourds chevaux qui ne henniront plus.
À midi le soleil ouvert comme un bouquet de paille
Sur les labours où leur buée erre encore en lambeaux,
S'englue et se débat longtemps dans la pulpe des raves.
Puis il descend en cahotant au bout du chemin creux,
De plus en plus gonflé sous son propre poids qui l'écrase,
Et perd dans chaque ornière une froide tige de feu.

FÉVRIER

Le vent nous a laissé la tristesse de la lumière.
L'horizon ploie ainsi qu'une clôture défoncée.
Sur le brasillement des bâches noires qui palpitent,
On cligne au soleil étourdi, trop tôt ressuscité,
Vague et mou dans des vêtements flottants comme ce souffle
En désordre par les labours qui n'auront pas dormi.

IMAGES FROM A PLATEAU

JANUARY

In the mud on the ridge path the frost
Has frozen the trails of the tipcarts whose rolling has stopped.
By the plateau's happy incline toss
The phantoms of the heavy horses whose neighing has stopped.
At noon the sun, open like a bouquet of straw
Over the plowed fields where shreds of mist roam,
Gets stuck and struggles a good while in the beets' pulp.
Then bumping and jolting it comes to the hollowed path's end,
More and more swollen under its own crushing weight,
And loses in each rut another cold fiery stem.

FEBRUARY

The wind left us light's sadness.
The horizon bends heavily like a staved-in wall.
On the glowing of the twitching black canvas sheets,
We blink at the absent-minded sun, too soon revived,
Vague and lifeless in clothing loose as this disorderly
Breath by the plowed fields that won't have slept.

MARS

Brusques les salves d'or et, dans la longue déchirure
D'air bleu, la cavalcade sabre au clair du petit bois
Chargeant à l'aile sans arrêt pour faire contrepoids
Au sombre enfoncement du centre où dès l'aube apparurent
Les lents lourds rangs profonds du gris en capote écrasant
Chaque motte, comblant tout les fossés, troublant l'eau claire
Et la vibration, sur l'eau, de la froide colère
Qui saisit l'herbe rase entre deux rafales de vent.

AVRIL

Ce qui vibre dans le cristal de l'air, c'est le mot même :
Avril, avec le frôlement des ailes des oiseaux,
Et les bords irisés du ciel paraissent trop fragiles
Pour contenir le bleu qui pétille sur les sillons.
La chaleur est comme une main qui nous touche l'épaule
Puis légère s'écarte et vient se poser sur le front,
Pendant qu'on cherche à découvrir, à moitié déjà saoule,
L'alouette qui boit à la source exultante du flot.

MARCH

Brusque the gold salvos and, in the long torn
Blue air, the cavalcade sabers through in the small wood's light
Endlessly charging the wing to balance out
The dark breaking through at the center where since dawn
The slow heavy deep ranks of grey in greatcoats appeared
Crushing each clump of earth, filling in all the ditches, clouding
The clear water and the vibration, on the water, of the cold anger
That seizes the short grass between two gusts of wind.

APRIL

It's the word itself that vibrates in the air's crystal:
April, with the rustling of birds' wings,
And the irised sky's edges too fragile
To contain the blue that sparkles on the plowed fields.
The heat is like a hand that touches us on the shoulder,
Then lightly withdraws and comes to settle on one's face,
While one strains to see the lark half drunk from the water
It takes in at the stream's exulting source.

MAI

Le vent s'est radouci puis changé sous les feuilles
En un chuchotement, et c'est celui du temps
Qui se repose au fond du berceau de la pluie
Avec le sommeil lourd et balancé des fleurs.
Le jour en panne flotte et lentement dérive
Jusqu'au ravin creusé par un soc de rayons
Qui se dressent le soir, tournant comme une roue
Que tire au ciel un délirant attelage d'oiseaux.

JUIN

Entre les haies qui se rejoignent en ogives
Et brillent ce matin comme un mur de vitraux
De vent, de ciel et d'or mêlés de neige vive,
Le chemin cesse d'avancer, pris d'engourdissement.
On le dirait hanté d'une invisible foule
Prête à chanter et dont les pas suspendus foulent
À peine une herbe droite et qui déjà l'entend.
À travers la chaleur qui s'élève en nuages
Et des épaisseurs de parfums acides ou sucrés,
On voit trembler au bout le plateau sans rivage,
Net et luisant comme un fragment d'éternité.

MAY

The wind has calmed then changed under the leaves
To a whisper, of time
Resting deep in the rain's cradle
With flowers' heavy, balanced sleep.
The broken-down day floats and slowly drifts
As far as the ravine dug by a plowshare blade of beams
That rise in the evening, turning like a wheel
Pulled in the sky by birds in a frenzied team.

JUNE

Between the hedges that join in arched ribs
And glow this morning like a stained-glass wall
Of wind, sky and gold mixed with vivid snow,
The path comes to a halt, overtaken with sleep.
You might say it's haunted by an invisible crowd
Ready to sing and whose suspended steps barely
Trample an upright lawn that already hears it.
Through the heat that rises in clouds
And thick layers of scents, acid or sugary,
The shoreless plateau can be seen trembling where the path ends,
Clear and gleaming like a fragment of eternity.

LA LUMIÈRE DE JUILLET

Au bout du chemin creux en berceau qui l'entoure
D'une auréole d'ombre où l'or s'est diffusé,
Elle reste assise sous un grillage d'herbes hautes,
Les mains sur les genoux que sa robe jaune découvre
Et les bras nus jusqu'à l'épaule, avec le cou ployé,
De sorte que l'on voit à peine son visage
Sous la paille brillante et souple de son chapeau.
Mais on sait qu'elle aussi nous voit. Elle s'engage
À présent dans ce tunnel sombre où, pour toucher sa peau
Profonde, nous allons, et pour effleurer ses cheveux
Tout à coup dénoués qui s'enflamment. Levant les yeux,
Elle nous fond complètement dans sa douceur aveugle.

AOÛT

Sous l'arpent de ciel vert et si vite fauché,
Le vent se ramifie en givre dans la luzerne,
Et ce geste pour embrasser encore la colline,
Le même : jamais plus. Cependant blonde et noire, la terre
Arrondit de nouveau sa hanche sous les épis,
Et contre elle j'attends que le jour qui s'éloigne verse
En criant comme un char de paille sur les talus.
Bleu le vent désencombre l'air à larges fourches
Au fond du val où deux golfeurs avancent par déclics
Entre les ombres des sapins qui poursuivent leur course
Et tournent insensiblement pour les saisir.

JULY LIGHT

At the end of the hollow cradle-like path that surrounds her
With a halo of shadow where gold has been diffused,
She stays seated under the tall grass's fine netting,
Her hands on the knees her yellow dress reveals
And her arms bare to her shoulders, with her neck bent,
In such a way that one barely sees her face
Under the glowing, supple straw of her hat.
But one knows she sees us too. Presently she
Enters this dark tunnel where, to touch that
Deep skin of hers, we go (and to lightly brush
Her hair suddenly undone now aflame). She lifts her eyes,
And within her blind gentleness utterly melts us.

AUGUST

Under the acre of green sky so quickly scythed,
The wind branches out as frost in the alfalfa,
And this gesture to embrace again the hill
Is the same: nevermore. Nonetheless blonde and black, the earth
Rounds out anew its hip under the ears of wheat,
And against the earth I wait for the disappearing day to pour
With a cry a kind of wagon of hay over the embankments.
Blue the wind clears large pitchforkfulls of air
At the valley's end where two golfers advance click by click
Between the shadows of the fir trees that follow their course
And turn imperceptibly to catch them.

SEPTEMBRE

La splendeur de septembre en marche surabonde
Sous ces branches où la lumière et l'épaisseur
Se reposent: lumière épaisse, épaisseur blonde,
Et le soir répandu plus loin dans sa douceur
Est rose avec des bois obscurs, des maisons claires,
Vallée ou plaine dans l'espacement des troncs,
Et la vague en suspens des coteaux circulaires
Levant un ciel doré qui pénètre les fronts.

OCTOBRE

Pylônes et pommiers par les plis vagues du plateau.
Il pleut sans bruit. Sans bruit, dans un lointain géologique,
Le pas plongeant d'un boeuf et la couronne de corbeaux
Mesurent un instant hors des siècles et des minutes.
Pylônes et pommiers avec le fil déchiré de cette eau
Me cousent tout au fond d'un jour sans ombre et sans limites.

SEPTEMBER

The splendor of September on the move overflows
Under these branches where thickness and light
Come to rest: blonde thickness, thick light,
And the widespread evening in its gentleness further off
Is pink with dark woods, bright houses,
Valley or plain within the trunks' spaces,
And the suspended wave of circular hills
Raising a golden sky that penetrates faces.

OCTOBER

Pylons and apple trees by the plateau's vague folds.
It's raining noiselessly. Noiselessly, in a geological distance,
A steer's plunging step and the crown of crows
Measure an instant beyond centuries and minutes.
Pylons and apple trees with this water's torn thread
Sew me deep within a day without shadows or limits.

NOVEMBRE

Retour, retour au lourd, au sourd, au compact, au placide
Dans la profondeur des couleurs où rien ne vibre plus,
Sauf à l'angle du bois un jet de rouille acide
Sous un coup de vent mou qui bat en tambour détendu.
L'odeur humide sourd du gris comme d'une fourrure
Et le ciel en rampant revient rouler sur les talus.
On enfonce la terre obscure et, de la même pâte
Épaisse mais dorée où le casque des freux reluit,
Un rayon tournant dans l'espace amorphe qu'il pétrit.

DÉCEMBRE

Depuis le matin vole une neige très fine
Mais vers le soir le vent s'étant mis à souffler
Il ne reste sur le plateau, le revers des collines,
Que des traces de blanc légèrement frotté
Et dans les creux une lueur aérienne de voile.
Chaque piquet de la clôture, à l'aplomb d'une étoile,
A l'air de savoir quelque chose ou d'attendre quelqu'un.
Mais les plus éloignés forment un long cortège
Qui se perd entre les replis des champs rouges et bruns
Et l'éclairement sourd des écharpes de neige.
On devine à peine les fils qui suivent le sentier
Filant au coin du bois vers le fond d'une combe
Pour reparaître sur la crête où, des nuages, tombent
Des lueurs qui le font resplendir comme un glacier.

NOVEMBER

Return to things placid, compact, heavy, mute,
In the pale colors' depths the motionless return
Except at the wood's corner a jet of acid rust
Under a lifeless gust of wind like a flat, slack drum.
The damp smell rises from the greyness as from a fur
And the creeping sky rolls on the embankment, returns.
The dark earth gets broken open and, of the same
Thick but golden stuff where the rooks' helmets gleam,
A turning ray in the amorphous space the light kneads.

DECEMBER

Since this morning a thin snow's been flying by
But towards evening the blowing wind
Left on the plateau, the hills' other side,
Mere traces of lightly rubbed white
And in the hollows a glimmer, a light, floating veil.
With starry assurance the fence's every pole
Appears to know something or be waiting for someone.
But a long procession is formed by those farthest off
And gets lost between the folds of fields red and brown
And the mute illumination of the snow's scarfs.
Following the path, the wires, but one barely sees them,
Winding at the wood's edge towards a combe's depth
To reappear on the ridge where, facing the clouds, the path
Meets the falling light and like a glacier now glistens.

DEUX SAISONS PARISIENNES

TWO PARISIAN SEASONS

L ' H I V E R   D E S   R U E S

P O N T   D E S   A R T S

À gauche la ville n'est plus un dédale de pierre,
Mais un très léger monument de cendre ou de poussière
Qui s'effondre sans bruit sous le poids du brouillard
Puis reparaît un peu plus loin, toujours plus vague,
Comme un rêve dans le sommeil bousculé d'un malade,
Entre les longues mains tâtonnantes des ponts.
Et j'avance parmi d'autres formes qui se défont
Sur la neige des quais, vers les jardins interminables.

THE WINTER OF STREETS

PONT DES ARTS

On the left the city is no longer a stone maze,
But the slightest of monuments of ash or of dust
That noiselessly collapses under the mist's weight
Then reappears further off, vague, indistinct,
Like a dream in a sick person's troubled sleep,
Between the bridges' long groping hands.
And among other forms come undone I advance
On the quais' snow, toward the endless gardens.

AU CANON DE MASSÉNA

Quelqu'un parle très loin dans l'épaisseur du temps
Et ses mots n'ont un sens précis dans aucune langue :
Ils font un peu dormir, ils apaisent, tout simplement.
Dehors un ciel distrait s'appuie aux façades qui réfléchissent.
Alors s'approchent rassurés les fantômes des grands
Cafés ancrés au bord de l'infini périphérique.
Ils écoutent parler ce type qui boit son blanc,
Hument la bonne odeur de tabac et de bière,
Parfois effleurant de leur lèvre invisible des verres
Où l'on voit un rond de buée aussitôt évanoui.
On se dit "c'est mon propre souffle qui passe
À travers l'eau dormante du jour d'hiver,
Avec ma vie".

AT THE MASSÉNA CANNON

Someone speaks far off in the thickness of time
In words that don't in any language quite seem to mean:
They bring on sleep, or simply calm.
Outside an absent-minded sky leans on the reflecting façades.
Then reassured they start to approach, the phantoms
Of the great cafés anchored on the infinite *périphérique* edges.
They take in the talk of this man sipping white wine,
Breathe in the sweet smell of tobacco and beer,
An invisible lip coming at times to lightly cover
A glass edge where a steam ring visibly subsides.
One says to oneself "it's my own breath gliding by
Across the winter day's sleeping water,
With my life."

LA MERCIÈRE

Ayant mis des chandails en solde sur le trottoir,
Elle contemple l'infini du fond de sa boutique.
Au passage on entend grésiller des musiques
Comme de l'huile chaude, au fond d'un petit transistor.
On croise en même temps des gens qui déménagent
Avec des poêles, des ballots débordant de lainages.
Ils ont l'air misérable et louche, un peu traqué.
Un couloir de travers les avale, et le pavé
Luit de nouveau comme un couteau dans un libre-service.
Froid et gras, son reflet met dans la profondeur
Des vitrines une autre rue où le ciel des tropiques
Décoloré voisine avec les fioles du coiffeur,
Des lavabos et des gâteaux aux couleurs utopiques.
Perdu bien au-delà sans remuer d'un cil,
L'oeil résigné de la mercière les traverse.
Elle n'attend plus rien. L'hiver est nuisible au commerce.
Elle ne vendra pas aujourd'hui la moindre bobine de fil.

THE SEWING NOTIONS DEALER

Having put sale sweaters outside on the corner,
She contemplates the infinite from inside her boutique.
Passing by one hears all sorts of crackling music
Like hot oil, within a small transistor.
One crosses paths at the same time with people moving out
With pans, with bundles overflowing with clothing.
They seem desperate and shady, a bit hunted down.
A crooked passage swallows them whole, and the cobblestone
Gleams again like a knife in a self-service restaurant.
Cold and slick, its reflection brings to the windows' depths
Another street where the bleached sky of the tropics
Is side by side with the hairdresser's flasks,
With sinks and cakes in colors utopian, aesthetic.
Lost well beyond without moving a lash, the resigned
Eye of the sewing notions dealer passes through all this.
She no longer awaits anything. Winter is bad for business.
Today she won't sell the least spool of thread.

NEIGE

La neige ne dit rien. N'est ici pour personne.
Un peu de nous s'annule aussi dans la blancheur.
Le crissement léger des pas qui ne résonnent plus
Contre les murs, cependant répéte au marcheur
Qu'il avance à travers l'espace blanc des rues
Sur la piste depuis longtemps oubliée ou perdue
Des hivers d'autrefois dont renaît la fraîcheur.
Mais il s'en va, broyeur indifférent d'étoiles,
La semelle épaisse d'un bloc déjà noir de cristaux :
Et pas deux semblables. Pas deux. La couche horizontale
Est comme un ciel amalgamant tous ses astres. Bientôt,
Des Africains frileux répandront du sel et du sable.
À peine la blancheur avait-elle tendu
Sa toile entre nos yeux et le fond insondable
Où tourbillonne cette neige obscure, un peu sanglante, du
Désir d'être, même en dormant, qui nous anime.
À peine entrés dans la paroi sans épaisseur,
De nouveau les remous, les jets du sel intime
Sur le voile immobile et vierge de la blancheur.

SNOW

The snow says nothing. Is here for no one.
Something of us cancels itself out as well in its whiteness.
The slight crunching of feet that no longer resonate
Against the walls, nonetheless repeats to he who walks
That he's advancing across the white space of streets
On the trail long since forgotten or lost
Of past winters from which coolness comes back to life.
But he goes off, an indifferent grinder of stars,
His sole thick with an already black block of crystals:
And no two alike. No two. The horizontal part
Is like a sky combining all that's seen from afar. Soon,
Africans sensitive to cold will spread salt and sand.
Barely had the whiteness hung
Its canvas between our eyes and the unsoundable depths
Where this obscure, somewhat bloody snow of desire for being
Even as we sleep animates us, swirls.
Barely entered within the inner wall without thickness,
Again the ebb and flow, the stream of intimate salts
On the still, virgin veil of whiteness.

LE REDOUX

Les moments où l'on perd ses contours et sa profondeur,
C'est souvent en hiver quand un souffle d'air tiède
Un peu hésitant flâne dans la rue. Une lueur
Rose passe à travers les nuages. Elle est à peine
Rose. On dirait plutôt un souvenir de la couleur,
Ou comme un effort indécis de rose qui renonce
Mais flotte encore et se mélange à tout ce dont soudain
On se rappelle. Et c'est le même instant qui recommence :
Le même instant, le même rose et la même douceur
De décembre; le même souffle en suspens dans l'espace
Prêt à s'ouvrir en nous, jusqu'à ce que plus rien
Ne demeure que cet instant qui passe et se souvient.

THE THAW

The moments when one loses one's contours and depth
Are often in winter when a breath of mild air hesitantly
Strolls in the street. A pink glow
Passes through the clouds. It's hardly
Pink. More like a memory of color,
Or as if an undecided effort at pink that gives up
But still floats and mixes with all that one
Suddenly recalls. And it's the same instant that up
And restarts: the same instant, the same rose, the same
December gentleness; the same suspended breath in space
Ready to open out within us, until there remains
Only this instant that passes and, itself, remembers.

PLACE VENDÔME

En bon ordre toujours et froids sur le velours céleste,
Dans la vitrine les bijoux brillent, peut-être faux.
L'air ganté de la nuit les palpe à travers le carreau
Puis tourne sur la place vide où, du même grand geste,
Il drape la colonne raide entre les chapiteaux.
Quand on passe comme le vent et qu'on lève la tête,
On distingue à l'étage, par de trop hautes fenêtres,
Des ombres et des coins dorés entre de lourds rideaux.
C'est l'autre face de la nuit, la caverne secrète
Avec les astres morts et la lune qu'on voit de dos
Dénombrer et polir des diamants et des cristaux.
On marche alors comme un voleur étonné qui pénètre
Dans la salle du coffre et sent que son propre cerveau
N'est qu'un chiffre du code impénétrable des planètes.

PLACE VENDÔME

In good order always and cold on the celestial velvet,
In the window the jewels glitter, perhaps fake.
The night's gloved air touches them through the pane
Then turns on the empty place where, with equal grace,
It drapes the taut column amid the capitals. When
One passes like the wind and raises one's head,
There, through too-high windows, one takes in
Shadows and gilded corners amid heavy curtains.
It's the other side of night, the secret cavern
With dead stars and the moon one sees from behind
Count and polish diamonds and crystals.
One walks then like a surprised thief who creeps
Into the safe-room and feels his own brain's
But a figure in the impenetrable code of planets.

LA MER

Un soleil fixe et blanc brille dans les ramilles,
Minces flammes brûlant devant le bleu puissant
Qui de l'autre côté des façades s'appuie
Sur une mer aux flots de menthe et de lilas.
Et cette mer on sait bien sûr qu'on l'imagine.
Mais peut-être suffirait-il de courir assez vite
Jusqu'au coin de la rue, et l'écume, le vent,
Tout l'espace écumant dans l'espace comme un taureau
Dont les cornes portaient la future lumière,
Bondiraient de nouveau comme par ces matins
Éblouis d'étincelles et de silence,
Quand nous étions les enfants préférés du soleil.

THE SEA

A fixed white sun shines in the small branches,
Thin flames burning before the strong blue
That from the other side of the façades leans
On a flowing mint and lilac sea.
And of course this sea is imaginary, clearly.
But maybe we'd just need to run quickly enough
To the corner of the street, and the froth, the wind,
All space lathering in space like a bull
Whose horns carried future light,
Would bound again as on those dazzled mornings
Of sparks and silence,
When we were the sun's preferred children.

LA BOULANGERIE

Souvent assez tard en hiver cette boulangerie
En face reste ouverte, et l'on peut voir le pain
Nimber d'or les cheveux frisés de la boulangère
Qui, bien qu'à tant d'égards ordinaire, nourrit
Des desseins obliques de femme et s'ennuie. Et parfois
La boutique à cette heure est vide; elle ne brille
Qu'à la gloire exclusive du pain.
Il suffit bien je crois de sa lumière au coin
De la rue assez tard en hiver pour que l'on remercie.

THE BAKERY

Often fairly late in winter this bakery
Across the way stays open, and one sees the bread
Circle with gold the shopgirl's curly hair,
The one who though unremarkable harbors
Oblique designs of womanhood and grows bored. And sometimes
The shop at this hour is empty; for the sole glory
Of bread it glows.
It's reason enough to give thanks I feel the shop's
Light by the street corner fairly late in winter.

C'EST LE PRINTEMPS

I

L'air s'élève comme un léger échafaudage
De pas, d'abois et de portes battant au fond sur des jardins
Verts dont le cri s'étouffe et m'atteint au passage,
Tandis que dans l'air je m'élève entre des rivières d'oiseaux
Vers le gris des nuages, le gris tantôt bleu, tantôt rose, aux
Roucoulements insituables de colombes. Et je l'écoute
Avec la douce explosion d'ailes sous les façades
Qui flottent dans le vent, qui s'ouvrent, et la croix
De la pharmacie au coin brille un peu plus encore, c'est le
    printemps.

II

De nuit ou juste avant que l'aube ait ouvert son ombrelle,
Tous les arbres de l'avenue ont d'un coup éclaté
Comme des bouteilles. Je marche au milieu des éclats,
Le front contre le vent, heurtant et recassant la vitre
Qui se reforme sur les toits en dôme transparent
Mais couvert d'une neige épaisse jusqu'au bleu qui brûle
Et dévale parmi les feux des branches, c'est le printemps.

IT'S SPRING

I

The air rises like a light scaffolding
Of steps, of baying and doors banging far off on green
Gardens whose cry dies out and reaches me while passing,
While in the air I rise amid rivers of birds
Toward the gray of clouds, the gray now blue, now pink, of doves'
Hard to place cooing. And I listen
With the gentle explosion of wings under the façades
That float in the wind, that open, and the cross
Of the corner pharmacy shines again a bit more, it's spring.

II

At night or just before the dawn has opened its parasol,
All the avenue's trees have at one go splintered
Like broken bottles. I walk among the splinters,
Face against the wind, hitting and breaking again the glass
Up on the roofs, a transparent dome reforming
But covered with a thick snow up to the blue that burns
And tumbles down amid the branches' fires, it's spring.

III

Pareil à ce jet d'eau que le vent ploie et disperse, qui
Pareil à la mort d'Absalon pareille à la sombre énergie
Du ciel, redevient ce jet d'eau paisible pareil à moi
Qui tourne sans bouger dans l'éternité du manège
Sous le haché menu tout frais des feuilles, des oiseaux,
Des cris d'enfants et des reflets du bassin pareil à
La rumeur lumineuse en ronds dispersés d'une foule
Où tout à coup le faune en bronze et qui danse, d'un pas
De trop se perd dans son ombre qui tourne, c'est le printemps.

IV

Quelqu'un loin dans le temps, dans la chaleur, enfonce un clou,
Puis on entend ronfler un petit moteur électrique
Et l'on s'endort un peu houspillé par les oiseaux.
Ils s'envolent muets entre les tentures de rêves
À nouveau décousus. J'ai la bouche et les yeux
Remplis de feuilles qui frémissent. Dans la cour,
Un coup de vent saisit et retrousse le lilas blanc
Qui fuit dans tous les sens comme une noce prise
De panique, c'est le printemps.

III

Like this fountain spray that the wind bends and disperses, that
Like the death of Absalom like the sky's dark energy,
Becomes again this peaceful fountain spray like myself
Who turns without moving in the carousel's eternity
Under the fresh broken menu of leaves, of birds,
Of childrens' cries and of the basin's reflection like
The luminous hum in dispersed rings of a crowd
Where all of a sudden the bronze dancing faun with one step
Too many gets lost in its shadow that turns, it's spring.

IV

Someone far off in time, in the heat, drives in a nail,
Then one hears a small electric motor purr
And one falls asleep somewhat scolded by the birds.
They fly off silent between the curtains of again
Disjointed dreams. My mouth and eyes
Are filled with trembling leaves. In the courtyard,
A gust of wind grabs and rolls up the white lilac
Fleeing in all directions like a panicked
Wedding party, it's spring.

V

Qui donc cogne si loin, si près, si doucement?
Ouvrez-lui, c'est peut-être
Le boucher Salomon contre un os sur sa table creusée
En oreiller sanglant; peut-être
Tout au fond de la cour ombreuse, y décerclant
Des fûts, Auguste l'épicier qui me captivait quand
Il racontait comment son casque à plumet et crinière
Était tombé dans la Vezouze un beau soir du printemps
1912. Il faut leur ouvrir cette porte aux serrures
De fer noir et d'oiseaux, car c'est eux,
C'est bien eux, j'en suis sûr, qui frappent et qui disent
Comme autrefois là-bas : Jacques, c'est le printemps.

VI

À Lyon je suis allé réciter des poèmes
Avec la contrebasse et la clarinette
Basse. Le ciel au retour traînait bas
Ses flancs gonflés sur la Saône, ses pans
À travers le Morvan jeté comme un manteau
De drap sombre devant les vignes, les colzas
En fanfare (je revoyais la porte ouverte
En avril au fond du garage). À Dijon,
Je suis resté coincé plus d'une heure par un orage,
À regarder la pluie arracher du béton
Des touffes de muguet en verre, et la glycine
Contre le mur du poste Esso fermé le jeudi, battre
Et battre. Une heure entière à me dire : c'est le printemps.

V

Who can that be banging so far, so close, so gently?
Let him in, it may be
Solomon the butcher against a bone on his hollowed
Bloody-pillow table; maybe
All the way back in the shady courtyard, unhooping
Casks, Auguste the grocer who used to captivate me when
He'd tell how his plume and mane helmet
Fell in the Vezouze one fine evening in spring
1912. This door with its locks of black iron and birds
Must be opened, for it's them,
It's definitely them, I'm quite sure, knocking and saying
As in the past there: Jacques, it's spring.

VI

In Lyon I went to recite poems
With double bass and bass
Clarinet. The sky on the way back dragged
Its swollen flanks low over the Saône, its patches
Across the Morvan thrown like a coat
Of dark sheet in front of the vines, the clamorous
Colzas (I pictured again the open door
In April in the back of the garage). In Dijon,
I got stuck for over an hour because of a storm,
Watching the rain tear concrete
From the glass lily of the valley clusters, and the wisteria
Against the wall of the Esso station closed Thursdays beat
And beat. An entire hour telling myself: it's spring.

VII

À six heures il pleut encore, une buée
Froide sort de la bouche obscure des marronniers,
Et mon reflet va devant moi, trouble sur le bitume,
Un peu fatalement, comme dans un vieux film.
À sept heures il pleut toujours. Le ciel respire
Dans les vitres des bâtiments déserts de la Poste. J'écris
Mon nom et mon adresse au dos de l'enveloppe. Il ne
Pleut presque plus. J'entends les jardins qui s'ébrouent, des pneus
Siffloter sur des airs de flûte. Une goutte
Perdue, en s'écrasant, fait de mon nom comme une fleur
Dont le bleu s'est éteint dans un livre, c'est le printemps.

VIII

Nous passons en causant tout bas sous les arbres. Ce merle
Nous écoute peut-être, car il s'est tu : les mots
Font un autre feuillage où quelque chose d'inconnu
Remue et le menace. Puis il recommence à chanter : nous passons,
Et quelque chose d'invisible, avec le cristal de sa gorge,
Flambe comme autrefois de plus loin qu'avant nous
Dans l'épaisseur du soir qui s'étonne, c'est le printemps.

VII

At six it's raining again, a cold mist comes out
Of the dark mouth of the chestnut trees,
And my reflection goes before me, clouds over the asphalt,
A bit dramatically, as in an old film.
At seven it's still raining. The sky breathes
In the deserted Post Office building windows. I write
My name and address on the back of the envelope. It's
Hardly raining now. I hear the gardens shaking dry, tires
Whistling a tune for flute. A lost
Drop, as it flattens, makes my name a kind of flower
Whose blue has gone out in a book, it's spring.

VIII

We pass by chatting softly under the trees. This blackbird
Is perhaps listening to us, for it's gone silent: the words
Make other foliage where something unknown
Threatens, stirs. Then it starts to sing again: we pass,
And something invisible, with the crystal of his throat,
Blazes as in the past from further ahead than in front of us
In the evening's thickness pleasantly surprised, it's spring.

IX

La chaleur, soudain la chaleur.
La chaleur comme une autre mémoire
Où l'on pourrait toucher vraiment les souvenirs
Comme des lèvres, comme un corps
Tout entier découvert dormant dans la chaleur
Qui se souvient aussi de mes lèvres. Le square
Est vide. Tout autour,
Les fenêtres obscures brandissent
Des rameaux éclatants de musique
Aussitôt confondus avec le silence du paulownia
Brûlant dans la chaleur son butane suave, c'est le printemps.

X

Ce soir c'est encore un soleil très blanc comme en novembre
Qui se dévêt timidement dans les feuilles, entre les corps
Bronzés et puissants des immeubles, touchant
Du bout du doigt l'eau du soir un peu froide. Un éclair
Plonge et d'un coup de reins se retourne. On voit
Briller son ventre et ses jambes. Du vent
Nage aussi par secousses d'un arbre à l'autre
Et sort en s'ébrouant à l'angle ébloui qui frissonne
Avec la bâche bondissante du Tabac.
Quelle heure est-il? Déjà. Mais le jour continue
À envahir la nuit, ainsi qu'un fleuve épais et lent
Qui s'enfonce loin dans la mer et repousse en aveugle
Un soleil aussi pâle et plat qu'un poisson mort.
Mais d'un soupirail éclairé sous le mur de l'orage,
S'échappe et fuit de porte en porte un rayon nu
Que poursuit ce long voile rose, c'est le printemps.

IX

The heat, suddenly the heat,
The heat like another memory
Where remembrances could truly be touched
Like lips, like an entire
Body discovered sleeping in the heat
That likewise remembers my lips. The square
Is empty. All around,
The dark windows brandish
Branches blazing with music
Straightaway mistaken for the silence of the paulownia
Burning in the heat of its sweet butane, it's spring.

X

This evening yet another sun quite white as in November
Undresses timidly in the leaves, amid the buildings'
Strong bronzed bodies, touching
With its fingertip the slightly cold evening water. A flash
Plunges down and heaves itself around by its back. One sees
Its stomach and legs gleam. Wind
Swims in jolts as well from one tree to the next
And emerges shaking itself out at the dazzled corner
That trembles with the Tobacconist's leaping tarp.
What time is it? Already. But day continues
Invading night, as well as a thick, slow river
That disappears far off into the sea and blindly pushes away
A sun as pale and flat as a dead fish.
But from a small basement window under the wall of the storm,
From door to door a naked ray escapes and flees
Pursued by this long pink veil, it's spring.

XI

J'entends rôder par les jardins la population de la pluie.
Ces pieds nus infiniment doux qui semblent revenir
D'un pays oublié, passent en moi comme à travers
Le feuillage tout neuf d'un vieil arbuste,
Lilas ou cytise enfin redéplié sous le ciel gris
De la cour qui s'enfonce avec la tourterelle
Au fond d'autrefois sous la pluie.
Je ne sais pas qui se souvient de visages mouillés,
Tendres comme des fleurs dans les branches qui ploient à peine
Sous ces pas innombrables. Je suis
L'espace où la douceur ancienne s'approche, l'herbe
Dont chaque brin porte une goutte où l'instant et le ciel
Et les jardins sont enfermés comme dans une perle
D'éternité mais qui tremble, c'est le printemps.

XII

C'est au coin de la rue, un soir
En apparence humide et froid comme les autres,
Qu'on a perçu dans l'air un soupir de chaleur plus profond.
Et dans le gris maussade, entre deux rafales de vent,
Quelqu'un nous a frôlés un instant mais sans hâte,
Étourdis par l'odeur soudain palpable des tilleuls.
Alors juste au coin de la rue on a vu disparaître
Celui dont on disait hier encore : c'est le printemps.

XI

I hear roaming through the gardens the population of the rain.
These infinitely gentle bare feet that seem to be returning
From a forgotten land pass within me as through
The brand new foliage of an old shrub,
Lilac or laburnum at last unfolded again under
The courtyard's gray sky that plunges with the turtledove
Deep within the past under the rain.
I don't know who recalls wet faces,
Tender as flowers in the branches that hardly bend
Under these countless feet. I'm
The space where the ancient gentleness approaches, the grass
Whose every blade carries a drop where the instant and the sky
And the gardens are enclosed as within a pearl
Of eternity but which trembles, it's spring.

XII

It's at the street corner, on an evening
Outwardly humid and cold like the others,
That we noticed in the air a deeper sigh of heat.
And in the sullen gray, between two gusts of wind,
Someone lightly brushed us an instant but unhurriedly,
Dazed as we were by the lindens' suddenly palpable smell.
Then just at the street corner we saw disappear
He about whom we were saying only yesterday: it's spring.

ÉCOLES DU SOIR

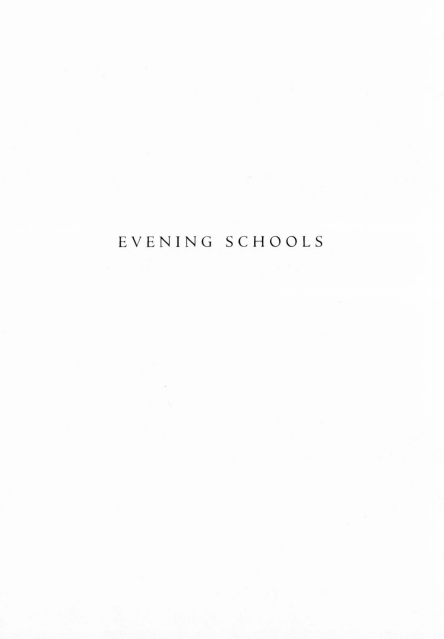

EVENING SCHOOLS

TARD EN AVRIL

Tout s'immobilisait sous le poids de la roue
Qui nous porte vers l'ombre avec nos battements de cils
Et nos cris si légers dans la lumière déclinante
Où s'élève en silence l'oiseau d'avril.
On n'entendait plus les enfants dans le fond du verger,
Ni les arbres tenir le temps en équilibre
Entre les rayons allongés du ciel bas à nos livres,
Et l'on vit les degrés du soir faciles s'étager
Pour le trébuchement du plus petit vers la douceur
Illusoire qui brille encore un peu sous les feuillages
Avant de consentir à la puissance de la nuit.

LATE IN APRIL

Everything came to a halt under the weight of the wheel
That carries us toward darkness with our eyelids beating
And our cries so faint in the declining light
Where the bird of April rises in silence.
We no longer heard the children in the orchard's depths,
Nor the trees keep time balanced
Amid the low sky's rays lying stretched out at our books,
And we saw the evening's ready degrees rise in terraces
For the smallest one's stumbling toward the illusory
Gentleness that still shines a bit under the foliage
Before consenting to the night's strength.

ASILE

Paix dans les petits pas en rond par le jardin,
Dans le durcissement de la cornée et la lente idiotie.
Le long du mur où le soleil étroit tient compagnie,
On est bien, le soir, on est bien.

*

D'une vie entière le soir basculant dans l'oubli,
Ne reste que ce tremblement de la main sur la clé;
La même main qui si longtemps trembla d'avoir giflé
Un enfant jeté dans le vain tremblement de la lumière.

*

Chaque soir il attend qu'on l'appelle. Tant de chagrins.
Car je dors peu la nuit, dit-il, mais je ne souffre guère
Que de ce robinet qui chuinte toujours, au sixième
Où je suis près du ciel tendre et glacé qui ne souffre pas.

*

Le soir, avec leur canne, ils dessinent dans la poussière
Des figures aussi brouillées que les paraboles des astres.
Le ciel peut tourner à présent, ça ne leur fait ni chaud ni froid;
Ils roulent par instants ces globes sanglants qui s'éteignent.

*

Et mieux vaut ignorer ce qui bouge dans les buissons
À l'approche du soir, entre les murs trop blancs des chambres :
Les souvenirs à l'abandon qui rôdent et s'en vont
Discrets comme des visiteurs qu'on ne veut plus entendre
Ni jamais revoir – sauf peut-être, à l'écart, ceux qui sont
Devenus un nuage, un chat maigre, un oiseau.

RETIREMENT HOME

Peace in the small circular steps by the garden,
In the cornea's hardening and the slow idiocy.
Along the wall where the narrow sun keeps company,
It's grand, evenings, it's grand.

*

From an entire life the evening toppling into forgetting,
There remains only this trembling of the hand on the key;
The same hand that for so long trembled at having smacked
A child thrown into the vain trembling of light.

*

Every evening he waits to be called. So many sorrows.
For I sleep little at night, he says, but scarcely suffer
But from this tap that always hisses, on the sixth floor
Where I'm near the tender frozen sky that doesn't suffer at all.

*

Evenings, with their cane, they draw in the dust
Figures as muddled as the parabolas of stars.
The sky can turn now, they couldn't care less.
They roll at times these blood-red globes that go out.

*

And it's better not to know what moves in the bushes
At evening's approach, between the rooms' too-white walls:
The neglected memories that roam and go
Discrete as visitors one no longer wants to hear
Or ever see again — except perhaps, standing apart, those who've
Become a cloud, a thin cat, a bird.

L'AMOUR

À sept heures les femmes sont belles et fatiguées.
Elles sortent à flot des banques, des magasins.
Peu songent à l'amour encore, elles ne sont touchées
Que par le rayon qui descend sous les branches de juin.
Mais tout le poids de la douceur qui les habite
Passe dans leurs talons aigus et sèchement crépite
Comme une immense machine à écrire sur les pavés.
Et j'écoute au fond du jardin ce froissement d'étoffes
Qui se confond avec le vent brassant d'épaisses touffes
De fleurs contre l'oeil sans paupière et sans larmes du soir,
Jusqu'à l'heure où l'amour les prend et puis les abandonne.
Le ciel sombre est alors pareil à leur regard
Qui tient longtemps sa profondeur ouverte pour personne.

LOVE

At seven the women are beautiful and tired.
They come out in streams from the banks, from the stores,
As yet few dream of love, they're touched
Only by the ray that comes down under the June branches.
But all the weight of gentleness that inhabits them
Passes to their sharp heels and crackles drily then
Like a huge typewriter on the cobblestones.
And I listen to this rustling of fabrics off in the garden's
Distance that merges with the wind mixing thick clusters
Of flowers against the evening's lidless tearless eye,
Until the hour when love takes and then abandons
Them. The dark sky is then like their gaze
That for a good while keeps its depth open for no one.

VERS L'ÉTOILE

En un clin d'oeil entre les murs, par la porte qui s'ouvre,
Le ciel rouge très sombre sous les branches qui veillaient,
Et puis quelqu'un (je n'ai rien vu) fuyant sous cette rouge
Lueur vers la cabane au fond (je n'ai rien vu : je sais).
Des gens que je n'ai pas connus traversent dans ces rues
Ma tête qui s'échappe et cogne et roule Dieu sait où,
Raflant des souvenirs tombés d'autres têtes. D'un coup,
J'aurai compris devant le feu de la coutellerie,
Qu'une femme de Brest avait un instant rêvé là
De la rade obscure, aux bateaux amarrés sous la pluie.
Et vingt pas encore : plus rien, plus personne. L'éclat
Des lames dans la nuit fuyait au fond des têtes vides.
Mais quelle autre image perdue alors m'attend au coin,
Sous la paille qu'au pied d'un sourd lampadaire la pluie
Remue? Et toujours je m'éloigne au bord de ces jardins,
Le long des murs, dans la douleur qui devient douce et froide
Et, dans l'ombre comme une tête où passent des remous,
Voilà cette autre porte encore ouverte et, tout au bout,
Le ciel rouge très bas surpris contre une palissade
Avec l'étoile nue et tremblante sur les cailloux.

NEAR L'ÉTOILE

In the blink of an eye between the walls, by the door that opens,
The dark red sky under the branches that kept watch,
And then someone (I saw nothing) fleeing under this faint red
Light toward the shed in back (I saw nothing: I know).
People I haven't met cross in these streets
My head which slips off and bangs and rolls God knows where,
Running off with memories fallen from other heads. Before
The fire of the cutlery store, I'll have quickly understood
A woman from Brest had briefly dreamed
There of the darkened harbor, its boats moored under the rain.
And another twenty steps: nothing else, not a soul. The blades'
Night brilliance fled back into empty heads.
But what other image lost then awaits me at the corner,
Under the straw that at the foot of an oblivious lamppost the rain
Shifts? And I keep moving off at the edge of these gardens,
Along the walls, in the pain that becomes gentle and cold
And, in the darkness like a head where swirls happen in,
Here's this other door open again and, at the far end,
The low red sky surprised against a palisade
With the naked trembling star on the stones.

LE SOIR D'HIVER

À quatre heures déjà le soir enfile son manteau
De ce ton vague entre mastic, nuages et poussière
Et s'avance furtivement dans la rue. Aussitôt,
Même ceux qui depuis le matin ne se soucièrent
De rien (croyant le jour normal ou peut-être éternel)
Se hâtent : on les voit marcher vers la phosphorescence
Qui grandit à chaque rond-point comme, au bout du tunnel,
La promesse d'un nouveau jour. Et tandis qu'ils recensent
Tous les signes certains de ce renversement — la cour
Crépitante comme un brasier d'oiseaux qui ressuscite;
Ce reflet rose entre leurs mains — le soir étonné court
Se recueillir sous des piliers plus noirs que l'anthracite :
Il doute si c'est lui qui pose ainsi sur l'épaisseur
Une clarté partout si limpide, que l'avenue
Les toits et les arbres touchés d'un rayon précurseur
Dressent une autre ville sous une étoile inconnue.
Et l'ombre de plus en plus dense à mesure, pourtant
Flotte encore, voile après voile envolés et qui laissent
À chaque fois l'illusion qu'on pourrait d'un instant
À l'autre basculer dans un intervalle céleste
Et se faufiler au-delà, par un long corridor,
Vers des collines se hissant du tréfonds le plus sombre
Dans un ruissellement de bleu sur des feuillages d'or.
Mais à l'écart l'irréparable est commis : le jour sombre,
Et le soir à son tour fuit les flegmatiques tueurs
De la nuit qui procèdent vite et bien, angle par angle
Où se cramponnent en tremblant les dernières lueurs :
Ils les entraînent sous un porche obscur et les étranglent.
Il ne reste plus pour cet homme en arrêt sur un pont

THE WINTER EVENING

At four already the evening puts on its coat, vaguely
Colored in that hue between putty, clouds and dust,
And advances furtively in the street. Straightaway,
Even those who since this morning cared about
Nothing (thinking the day normal or perhaps eternal)
Hurry: one sees them walk toward the phosphorescence
Which grows at each roundabout as, at the end of the tunnel,
The promise of a new day. And while they make inventory lists
Of all the sure signs of this reversal – the crackling
Courtyard like an inferno of birds that resuscitates;
This pink reflection between their hands – the astonished evening
Runs to gather its thoughts under pillars darker than anthracite:
Has doubts whether it's he who sets thus on the thickness
A clear light everywhere so limpid, that the avenue
The roofs and the trees touched by a ray that anticipates
Raise another city under an unknown star.
And the shadow, increasingly dense as things go, still
Somehow floats, veil after veil blown off and each leaves
The illusion that one could from one instant
To the next topple over into a celestial distance
And thread one's way beyond, by a long corridor,
Toward hills heaving themselves up from darkest inmost depths
In a stream of blue on leaves made of gold.
But off to the side the irreparable is committed: the day sinks,
And the evening in turn flees the night's phlegmatic killers
Who proceed quickly and well: angle by angle
Where trembling the last lights cling before
Being dragged off under an obscure porch, then strangled.
There remains for this man under a bridge, stopped,

Qu'une barre glacée à l'horizon mais qui fulgure
Et, cependant que tout s'éteint autour de lui, répond
Au feu sourd qui paraît nimber encore sa figure.

Only a frozen bar on the horizon but that offers a brief blaze
And, while around him all goes out, responds
To the muted fire that appears to still encircle his face.

CÈDRE À MEUDON

Tout au fond du jour en poussière et silence d'archives
Un cèdre s'est haussé dans l'air par vagues successives,
Étales désormais entre deux abîmes du temps.
Chacune porte un souvenir, et mes pas hésitants
Semblent entrer dans la mémoire obscure de ce cèdre
Planant sur les collines de Clamart et de Meudon.
De versant en versant tous semblables, où l'on pense être
Enfin perdu, veille le même oiseau sagace dont
Le chant creuse l'écho d'un autre chant sous l'étendue.
Et c'est comme autrefois quand, dans une heure confondue
Au miel céleste ruisselant jusque sur le guidon
Chromé du vélo rouge, on s'arrêtait soudain à cause
Du même chant venu déjà d'un fond plus ancien
Ou futur, à jamais futur, perdu comme ce chien
Qui semble enfermé dans l'effroi d'une métempsycose
Et qui flaire entre les jardins la trace de l'oubli.
On trouve alors, dans les sentiers que l'ombre ensevelit
Et qui se trompent, un couloir où n'ose aller personne,
Comme dans ces villas aux volets branlants qu'on soupçonne
De savoir, là, debout sur leur talus philosophal,
Pourquoi la nuit s'approche à petits bonds au flanc du val.

CEDAR AT MEUDON

Far back in the dusty day silent as archives
A cedar raised itself up in the air in successive waves,
Since then gone slack between two depths of time.
Each wave carries a remembrance, and my hesitant steps seem
To enter this cedar's obscure memory
Hovering over the hills of Clamart and Meudon.
Along slopes that all resemble each other, where finally
You feel lost, a shrewd bird keeps watch, the same whose song
Hollows out the echo of another song under the expanse.
And it's like days long past when, in an hour mixed
With the celestial honey streaming up to the red bike's chrome
Bars, you'd suddenly stop because
Of the same song come already from a more ancient depth
Or future, forever future, lost like this dog
That seems trapped in the fear of a metempsychosis
And that sniffs between the gardens at forgetting's trace.
It's then you find, in the footpaths that shadow shrouds
And that err, a passage no one dares enter,
As in these villas with loose flapping shutters you expect
To know, standing there on their philosopher's bank,
Why the night approaches in small bounds at the valley's flank.

MAISONS À MALAKOFF

Comme ces herbes dont on ignore le nom
(On dit : de l'herbe; à peine ont-elles des racines
Et quelquefois des fleurs d'un modeste linon),
Au bord de leurs jardins encombrés de bassines
Les petites maisons se dressent dans l'air cru
Du soir qui fait monter la flamme de leurs teintes :
Ocre rouge, safran, azur ou pâle écru,
Puis cet or infusé des vitres où des têtes
Énormes, pour ne rien briser, très lentement
Bougent. Mais préservant un équilibre instable,
Ces maisons où tout n'est que rétrécissement
Semblent porter le ciel posé comme une table.
Et la douceur se tient muette par-dessous
Dans une vigilante étreinte de clôtures,
Car le temps et l'espace enfin se sont dissous
L'un l'autre comme au fond des paisibles peintures.
Il suffit d'avancer alors encore un peu,
Sans produire le plus léger mouvement d'onde,
À travers la substance impalpable qui peut
Devenir, aux chantiers Vidal-et-Champredonde,
Ferraille, ou tour de bronze à l'horizon barré
D'un long mur gris suave où toutes les nuances
Et les lignes rompant le jeu des confluences
Dorment : le monde obscur et vide est éclairé.

HOUSES AT MALAKOFF

Like those grasses with hard to know names
(We say: grass; they hardly have roots
And sometimes flowers of modest fine linen),
At the edge of their gardens cluttered with basins
The small houses stand up in the harsh evening air
That brings out the flame of their tints:
Red ochre, saffron, azure or pale ecru,
Then this infused gold of windows where enormous heads,
To break nothing, very slowly move.
But preserving an unstable balance,
These houses where all is shrinking and narrow
Seem to carry the sky set up like a table.
And the gentleness keeps silent below
In a vigilant embrace of walls,
For time and space have finally dissolved
Each other as deep within peaceful paintings.
It's enough then to advance a bit more,
Without producing a wave movement ever so slight,
Through the impalpable substance that appears
It may become, at the Vidal-et-Champredonde building sites,
Scrap iron, or a bronze tower on the blocked horizon
Of a long soft-gray wall where all nuances
And lines breaking the play of confluences
Sleep: the dark empty world is enlightened.

LE PRIX DE L'HEURE DANS L'ÎLE SAINT-GERMAIN

Les ombres des passants s'allongent à vue d'oeil,
Marquant l'heure cosmique en travers des pelouses.
Aussi chaque brin d'herbe a son ombre qui bouge
Comme l'aiguille d'un très sensible appareil.
Mais d'en haut, au sommet du large monticule,
Cette agitation demeure imperceptible. Un grand
Arbre déjà rougi par l'automne spécule
Solitaire au milieu de son vaste cadran.
De l'or pulvérisé tombe sur la colline :
À mesure que le soleil pâle décline,
Ce brouillard triomphal auréole Meudon
Puis un jeune passant qui répète : "Pardon,
Monsieur, n'auriez-vous pas deux francs, deux francs cinquante?"
Tenant de l'autre main sa valise à brocante,
Il attend. Et je m'exécute. Encore un franc.
Je pense qu'il ira les fumer ou les boire.
Si l'on nous aperçoit depuis l'Observatoire,
Nous devons avoir l'air, dans le soir de safran,
D'un groupe antique et sur le point de faire un pacte.
En échange, de fait : "Avez-vous l'heure exacte?"
Ai-je cru devoir dire alors qu'il s'éloignait.
D'un geste las il a découvert son poignet :
Rien. Mais sur l'herbe, un peu plus tard, son ombre oblique
Donnait l'heure (elle était juste et mélancolique).

THE PRICE OF TIME AT THE ÎLE SAINT-GERMAIN

The shadows of passers-by lengthen before one's eyes,
Marking the cosmic hour across the lawns,
Giving each blade of grass its shadow that moves
Like the needle of a quite sensitive device.
But from above, at the large hillock's summit,
This restlessness remains imperceptible. A great
Big tree already reddened by autumn speculates
Alone in the middle of its vast dial's face.
Powdered gold falls on the hill:
As the pale sun declines,
This triumphal mist crowns Meudon
Then a young passer-by who repeats: "Excuse me, Sir,
You wouldn't happen to have two francs, two francs fifty?"
Holding in his other hand his flea market bag, he
Waits. And I pay up. Another franc.
I think he'll go smoke or drink them.
And if from the Observatoire we're seen,
We probably seem, in the saffron evening,
Like a group from antiquity about to make a pact.
In exchange, in fact: "Do you have the exact
Time?" I felt I should say as he walked into the distance.
With weary mime he revealed his wrist:
Nothing. But on the grass, a bit later, his oblique
Shadow gave the time (it was true and melancholic).

LA LUMIÈRE À CHÂTILLON

Ce sont les petites maisons pleines d'heures perdues
Entre les vergers devenus sauvages, les lilas,
Et le ciel encombré de nuages qui descend bas,
Pâle d'avoir usé son bleu contre ces étendues.
Et j'avance à mon tour parmi les feuillages trempés
Dont les verts éclatants ou tendres mais fous se mélangent,
Et laissent entrevoir soudain la perspective étrange
De Montmartre ou de Courbevoie aux versants escarpés
Comme s'ils se dressaient tout juste après la palissade,
Si proches brusquement que l'on pourrait poser les doigts
Contre l'arête d'une tour, au bord d'une esplanade,
Dans la cendre qui tremble bleue et rousse sur les toits.
Me voici du côté de la véritable lumière
Que j'avais déjà découvert autrefois en dormant.
Je reconnais chaque chemin, chaque arbre, chaque pierre,
Mais je les vois pour la première fois; l'étonnement
Me soulève de rue en rue; une vague mémoire
En même temps s'éveille : ici j'ai vécu, je vivrai
De toute vie au fond des jardins, des chambres (il faut croire
Ce que je dis, car c'est le soir qui parle et qui dit vrai).

THE LIGHT AT CHÂTILLON

They're the small houses full of lost hours
Among orchards grown wild, the lilacs,
And the sky cluttered with clouds that comes down low,
Pale from having worn away its blue against these expanses.
And I advance in turn amid the drenched foliage,
With its greens bright or tender but gone mad that mix
And suddenly allow a glimpse of the strange perspective
Of Montmartre or Courbevoie with their steep slopes
As if they were rising sharply just after the palisade,
So close all of a sudden you could place your fingers
Against a tower's crest, at the edge of an esplanade,
In the ash that trembles blue and russet on the roofs.
Here I am on the side of the true light
That I'd already discovered in the past as I slept.
I recognize each path, each tree, each stone, but
I see them for the first time; astonishment
Lifts me from street to street; a hazy memory
At the same time awakens: here I lived, through
All life I'll live within gardens, rooms (believe what I say,
For it's the evening that talks and speaks true).

DIEU À BERCY

Ces platanes l'été font des voûtes opaques
Pour la petite église ocre, sans badigeon,
Qui luit dans l'ombre au bout de la rue de Dijon
Où le hasard me reconduit, ce jour de Pâques.
Les feuillages ne font qu'un léger poudroiement
Entre le ciel du soir livide et les bâtisses
Des entrepôts déserts où des chats subreptices
Se faufilent entre les fûts. Un bon moment,
Je reste sous la colonnade entre Saint-Pierre
Et Saint-Paul, écoutant le silence total
Qui descend avec le soleil horizontal
Dont le feu blanc m'oblige à cligner la paupière.
Mais dans l'église rôde un murmure sans fin,
Doux comme les accents d'un ancien office,
Et j'entre alors timidement dans l'édifice
Vide. Il est vide, à part la voix de séraphin
Qui, sans aucun souci de l'ordre liturgique,
Entonne de nouveau ce motet de l'Avent
Où *nos iniquités nous ont comme le vent
Emportés.* Puis le *Consolamini*, si nostalgique
Qu'on croirait Dieu Lui-même en train de déplorer
L'enchaînement de cette inconcevable histoire
De colère, d'amour, de grâce aléatoire.
Et, comme au fond d'un recoin sale et dévoré
Par l'éternel néon d'une salle d'attente,
Il se tient loin de la lumière encore trop
Violente qui heurte à travers les vitraux
La statue en nickel de la Vierge, éclatante.

GOD AT BERCY

These plane trees in summer make opaque archways
For the small ochre church, without distemper,
That gleams in the shadow at the end of the rue de Dijon
Which chance takes me back to, this Easter day.
The foliage is only a thin dust haze
Between the pallid evening sky and the buildings
Of deserted entrepôts where cats, surreptitious,
Thread their way among the casks. I stay
A good while under the colonnade between Saint-Pierre
And Saint-Paul, listening to the total silence
That descends with the horizontal sun
Whose white fire obliges me to half close an eyelid.
But in the church an endless murmur roams,
Gentle as the tones of an ancient office,
And so I timidly enter the empty edifice.
Empty, but for the seraph voice
That, without any concern for the order of the liturgy,
Strikes up again this Advent motet
Where *our iniquities have like the wind*
Taken us away. Then the nostalgia of the *Consolamini,*
As if God Himself were in the middle of deploring
The events of this inconceivable story
Of anger, of love, of aleatory grace.
And, as if deep within a dirty nook devoured
By a waiting room's eternal neon,
He keeps far from the light, still so
Violent, that strikes through the windows
The radiant nickel statue of the Virgin.

LA BICYCLETTE

Passant dans la rue un dimanche à six heures, soudain,
Au bout d'un corridor fermé de vitres en losange,
On voit un torrent de soleil qui roule entre des branches
Et se pulvérise à travers les feuilles d'un jardin,
Avec des éclats palpitants au milieu du pavage
Et des gouttes d'or en suspens aux rayons d'un vélo.
C'est un grand vélo noir, de proportions parfaites,
Qui touche à peine au mur. Il a la grâce d'une bête
En éveil dans sa fixité calme : c'est un oiseau.
La rue est vide. Le jardin continue en silence
De déverser à flots ce feu vert et doré qui danse
Pieds nus, à petits pas légers sur le froid du carreau.
Parfois un chien aboie ainsi qu'aux abords d'un village.
On pense à des murs écroulés, à des bois, des étangs.
La bicyclette vibre alors, on dirait qu'elle entend.
Et voudrait-on s'en emparer, puisque rien ne l'entrave,
On devine qu'avant d'avoir effleuré le guidon
Éblouissant, on la verrait s'enlever d'un seul bond
À travers le vitrage à demi noyé qui chancelle,
Et lancer dans le feu du soir les grappes d'étincelles
Qui font à présent de ses roues deux astres en fusion.

THE BICYCLE

Passing in the street on a Sunday at six, suddenly,
At the end of a closed passage, its windows like diamonds,
One sees a torrent of sun that rolls between the branches
And turns to powder through a garden's leaves,
With quivering fragments in the middle of the cobbles
And, suspended from a bike's spokes, drops of liquid gold.
It's a large black bike, perfectly proportioned,
That hardly touches the wall. It has the grace of an intent
Animal in its calm steadiness: it's a bird.
The street is empty. The garden continues in silence
Pouring these streams of green and gold fire that dance
Barefoot, with small light steps on the pane's cold.
Occasionally a dog barks as if at the outskirts of a village.
One thinks of walls come down, of woods, of ponds.
The bicycle then vibrates, one might say it hears.
And if one were to grab it, since nothing keeps it chained,
One can well imagine, before even brushing its dazzling
Bars, seeing it in a single bound take
Off across the half-drowned glazing that wavers,
And casting in the evening's fire the clusters of sparks
That turn its wheels now into two glowing stars.

THÉSÉE À VAUGIRARD

Je ne sais qui ou quoi m'attend dans ce dédale
À vrai dire sans grand mystère où j'aime aller
Le dimanche ou le soir, quand la lueur égale
Se fige entre la rue et le ciel crénelé
De tuyaux et de toits dont les pentes décèlent
Des passages, des cours, des lambeaux de jardins,
Avec des voix et des tintements de vaisselle
Rendant plus épais le silence, et de soudains
Oiseaux qui font le cri de petites poulies
Sous un lierre flottant comme autour d'un puits noir,
Et le plâtre des murs couturé de scolies
Illisibles dans la pénombre des couloirs.
Mais c'est toujours la même histoire que j'éreinte,
Page à page quand tout en est depuis longtemps
Connu, comme le plan de ce faux labyrinthe
Où le soir me rappelle et cache qui j'attends.

THESEUS AT VAUGIRARD

I don't know who or what awaits me in this frankly
Unmysterious maze where I like to go
On Sundays or evenings, when the even light
Freezes between the street and the sky so
Crenelated with pipes and roofs whose slopes indicate
Passages, courtyards, scraps of gardens,
With voices and the clinking of plates
Making the silence thicker, and sudden birds
That cry out with the creak of small pulleys
Under ivy floating as if around a dark well,
And the wall plaster scarred with critiques
Unreadable in the half-light of the halls.
But it's always the same story I wear to bits,
Page after page when it's all long since clear,
Like the plan of this false labyrinth where it's
Evening that reminds me of and hides who I'm waiting for.

PASSANT

Je suis sûr que le monde avance avec mes jambes,
Pense avec mon cerveau, regarde avec mes yeux.
Combien de temps resterons-nous encore ensemble?
Et personne ne sait vraiment lequel des deux
Quitte l'autre, quand cette existence commune
S'achève sans commun accord. Et c'est pourquoi
L'âme et l'air sont déjà remplis d'une amertume
Lorsque marchant le soir avec son ombre, on voit
À chaque pas un peu du monde disparaître,
Un peu de soi glisser dans l'eau froide du temps.
Cependant à l'abri derrière leur fenêtre,
Des gens font retomber les rideaux, mécontents,
Comme si l'on voulait leur ravir le mystère
D'être des autres. Mais ils l'ignorent, bien sûr,
Et l'autre est le passant qu'un virage oblitère
Pour le rendre à l'indifférence d'un ciel pur.

PASSING BY

I feel sure the world advances with my legs,
Thinks with my brain, looks with my eyes.
How much time will we still stay together?
And no one truly knows which of us leaves
The other, when this common existence
Ends without common accord. And that's why
The soul and the air are already filled with a bitterness
When, walking in the evening with one's shadow beside,
One sees with each step a bit of world disappear,
A bit of oneself slide into time's cold water.
Meanwhile behind their window, shielded,
People let the curtains fall back down, bothered,
As if one wanted to rob them of the mystery
Of being others. But they are unaware of it, of course,
And the other is the passer-by whom a curve turns away
To return him to a pure sky's indifference.

L'ESPOIR DES RUES

Sait-on si c'est l'oiseau du soir ou de l'aurore
Qui chante quand demeure en suspens la clarté
Sur les maisons levant du fond de la mémoire
Leur front neuf contre un ciel encore inhabité
Mais où dans un moment les premières étoiles
Perceront, et la lune aussi mince qu'un fil?
Cependant l'air est plein, tendu comme la voile
D'un vaisseau ramenant en gloire de l'exil
Ces hauts toits entassés au-dessus de la rue
Qui se rappelle et qui titube entre ses murs,
Tandis que la grive s'apaise et que la crue
De lumière se heurte aux angles plus obscurs.
Pourtant la rue avance encore, elle est certaine
D'atteindre enfin le bout de la rue et d'ouvrir
Son dernier détour hésitant devant la plaine
Éblouie où le soir, aube du souvenir,
Monte.

THE HOPE OF STREETS

Do we know if it's the bird of evening or of dawn
That sings when the clearness remains suspended
Over the houses raising from the depths of memory
Their new face against a still uninhabited sky
But where in a moment the first stars will
Break through, and the moon as thin as a thread?
Meanwhile the air is full, taut as the veil
Of a vessel bringing back in glory from exile
These high roofs piled up above the street
That recalls and totters between its walls,
While the thrush grows peaceful and the flood
Of light collides with the darker angles.
Yet somehow the street still advances, it's certain
To finally reach the end of the street and open
Its last hesitant detour before the dazzled plain
Where the evening, the dawn of remembrance,
Rises.

LE JOUR DU SEIGNEUR

Le solitaire qui s'en va, sur le coup de cinq heures,
Par les rues calmes et déjà sombres sous un ciel gris,
Aime voir s'allumer sur la façade des immeubles
Et comme au hasard les fenêtres. C'est son répit,
La lente éclosion de ces fleurs jaunes et roses,
Quand le jour, sur le point de se retirer, pose
Au fond des squares un dernier regard écarquillé.
Il croit pouvoir redevenir lui-même, ou s'éveiller
Un autre à la lueur secrète où baigne chaque chambre,
Et s'y confondre avec tous ceux dont bouge à peine l'ombre
Derrière des rideaux qu'agite un souffle de chaleur
Qui les laisse engourdis sous le poids du silence.
Ainsi passe à travers les murs, à la fin du dimanche,
De lampe en lampe un invisible visiteur.

THE LORD'S DAY

The loner who heads off, at the stroke of five,
Along the calm and already dark streets under a gray sky,
Likes to see as if randomly the windows light
Up on the buildings' façades. It's his respite,
The slow opening up of these yellow and pink flowers,
When the day, about to take its leave, offers
At the far end of the squares a last wide-eyed look.
It thinks it can become itself again, or awake
As another by the secret glimmer where each room bathes,
And merge there with all those whose shadow hardly moves
Behind curtains a breath of warmth flutters
That leaves them sluggish under the weight of silence.
Thus passes through the walls, as Sunday comes to an end,
From lamp to lamp an invisible visitor.

LA COUTURE

Au fond de la cour bleue où les tilleuls remuent,
La vielle dame, en tablier noir et bleu, coud.
Tout semble juste ici quand on vient de la rue
Pourtant calme un dimanche, avec le ciel beaucoup
Plus profond et majestueux que d'habitude
Et qui s'évase entre les toits comme un large entonnoir
De lumière où s'absorbe un nuage. Le soir
Se rapproche. Mais l'heure est dans la plénitude
Où reposent en mai les longs après-midi
Quand, des arbres que rien encore n'inquiète,
Descend un froissement de pages qu'on feuillette
Et le râle voluptueux d'un ramier engourdi.
Je ne sais quelle porte au hasard j'ai poussée :
La dame en noir et bleu me regarde. Elle coud
Un juste pan d'ombre à la nappe éclaboussée
De soleil où je flotte. Et je sens tout à coup
Qu'elle et moi nous allons bientôt, si je m'attarde,
Nous reconnaître sans pouvoir franchir cette lézarde
Qui fuit sous les tilleuls en travers de la cour.

SEWING

At the back of the blue courtyard where the lindens stir,
The old woman, with a black and blue smock on, sews.
Everything seems right here when you come from the street
Actually calm on a Sunday, with the sky much deeper
And more majestic than usual,
And between the roofs like a large funnel flaring
With light within which a cloud is absorbed. The evening
Approaches. But the hour is in the plenitude
Within which rest in May the long afternoons
When, from the trees that nothing yet worries,
There descends a rustling of leafed-through pages
And the voluptuous groan of a sluggish pigeon.
I don't know what door I randomly pushed:
The woman in black and blue looks at me. She sews
An apt patch of shadow on the sheet splattered
With sun where I float. And all at once
I feel she and I we'll soon, if I linger,
Recognize each other without being able to get past this fissure
That flees under the lindens crosswise through the courtyard.

L'ARC-EN-CIEL

Un vent chaud en avril nous dit qu'il est possible
D'être mort quand le ciel se couvre et que les toits dorés
Pèsent légèrement le soir sur la fatigue
Dans la rue où l'on va parmi d'invisibles fourrés.
Comme échappés d'un bond à des portes qui battent,
Des éclairs convulsifs éclatent sur les fronts
Et, contre un laurier dont la tête heureuse encense, quatre,
Cinq, six gouttes de pluie ainsi qu'un petit balafon
Tintent. Je ne sais plus de quel côté je marche.
Le vent me traverse et je suis le vent et les oiseaux,
Puis ce doux roulement de tonnerre sous l'arche
Lumineuse qui s'arrondit au-dessus des maisons.

THE RAINBOW

A warm wind in April tells us it's possible
To be dead when the sky clouds over and the golden roofs
Weigh slightly in the evening on the fatigue
In the street where one goes amid invisible thickets.
As if escaped with a bound from doors that strike,
Convulsive flashes of lightning burst on faces
And, against a laurel whose happy head sprinkles incense,
Four, five, six drops of rain plus a small balafon
Chime. I no longer know which side I'm walking on.
The wind crosses through me and I'm the wind and the birds,
Then this gentle rumbling of thunder under the luminous
Arch that rounds and swells above the homes.

UN PARADIS D'OISEAUX

A PARADISE OF BIRDS

LE GEAI

C'est au creux d'un vallon fermé comme une boîte
Où l'automne avait mis un épais tampon d'ouate
Étouffant dans les bois l'aboi de chiens sanglants,
Qu'au-dessus de Limours j'ai recueilli ces glands
Pour le geai réputé farouche et difficile
Et qui n'en a pas moins élu pour domicile
À Paris un des grands platanes de ma cour.
Le matin quelquefois on l'entend qui discourt
Avec sa fougue acariâtre de crécelle,
Mais du bleu sous le brun de sa bure étincelle
Et rouvre l'oeil en or insondable des chats.
Je l'ai vu qui piquait sur leurs ronds de pachas
Roux et gris se donnant une allure distraite.
À la fin cependant ils battent en retraite
Jusque sous les fusains puis, en catimini,
Ils guettent de nouveau le feuillage où le nid
Se dissimule. Mais, je dois le reconnaître,
J'ai souvent soutenu l'oiseau, de ma fenêtre,
En projetant sur ces félins divers objets.
Faut-il aider aussi les victimes des geais
Et, de fil en aiguille avec cette logique,
Intervenir dans le déroulement tragique
D'une histoire où toujours un mangeur est mangé?
Mais qui mange du chat, d'habitude? Si j'ai
Humé plus d'une fois, sur des tables chinoises,
Des ragoûts aux saveurs légèrement sournoises,
Ce ne fut qu'une entorse à l'ordre naturel.
Nous-mêmes, c'est le temps qui nous mâche et nous ronge;
Les dieux mangent du temps, mangés par le mensonge

THE JAY

It's in the hollow of a small valley closed like a box
Where autumn had put a thick cotton tampon stop
In the woods to the bark of bloody dogs,
That above Limours I gathered these acorns
For the jay reputed to be difficult and wild
And that nonetheless established domicile
In a large plane tree in my courtyard in Paris.
In the morning sometimes one hears it chatter
With its sour fiery spirit like a rattle,
But some blue under the brown of its frock sparkles
And reopens the unfathomable golden eye of the cats.
I saw it stabbing at the rounds these russet and gray
Pashas were making pretending to be distracted.
Ultimately though they beat a retreat
As far as the spindle-trees then, on the quiet,
They intently watch again the foliage where the nest
Conceals itself. But, I do admit,
I've often backed the bird, from my window,
By throwing at these felines various objects.
Must we also help the victims of the jays
And, gradually following this logic,
Intervene in a story and its unfolding, tragic,
Wherein an eater is always eaten?
But who usually eats cat? If I've breathed in
More than once, when eating Chinese,
Somewhat insidiously flavored stews,
It was only a break from the natural order.
Us, it's time that chews us, eats us away;
The gods eat time, eaten by lies

(Mais ne nous perdons pas dans cet universel.
Que mon poème soit un simple grain de sel
Sur la queue agile du geai, quand il m'honore
De son éclair céleste et de son cri sonore).

(But let's not lose ourselves in things universal.
May my poem be a simple grain of salt
On the jay's agile tail, when it lets me take pride
In its celestial flash and sonorous cry).

LA PIE

Au nouvel habitant de la cour (une pie) :
Derrière mon rideau, ma vieille, je t'épie,
Car depuis ce matin – et ce n'est pas fini –
Tu n'as pas arrêté d'aller, venir : ton nid
Doit prendre forme en haut de l'immense platane,
Avec des ramillons, des bouts de tarlatane,
De paille, de ficelle; et, régulièrement,
On entend éclater ton sec ricanement
Qui suspend à tout coup la cadence baroque
Du merle et, des moineaux, l'effervescent colloque.
Le concert matinal deviendra bien succinct
Quand, ta famille ayant passé de deux à cinq,
La cour, déjà soumise aux rauques tourterelles,
Retentira du bruit sans fin de ses querelles.
Il est vrai que dans le blason des animaux,
Rien ne vaut la sobriété des deux émaux
Qui, composant le tien d'argent pur et de sable,
Te rendent entre mille oiseaux reconnaissable,
Comme ce vol au mécanique et lourd ballant
Qui paraît imiter celui d'un cerf-volant.
Certains, bien avant moi, qui t'avaient admirée,
Ont dit que tu marchais en habit de soirée,
Élégante et maligne ainsi qu'on a dépeint
Cet autre convoiteur d'étincelles, Lupin.
Car on te sait de plus chapardeuse, méchante,
Et tu chantes vraiment trop mal pour qu'on te chante
Autrement que je fais. Aussi vaudrait-il mieux,
Agasse, qu'au plus tôt tu désertes ces lieux,
Avant qu'un riverain moins calme ne combine
De t'en persuader avec sa carabine.

THE MAGPIE

To the courtyard's new inhabitant (a magpie):
From behind my curtain, my dear, closely I
Watch, for since this morning – without rest –
You keep coming, going: your nest
Must be taking shape on top of the huge plane,
With twigs, bits of muslin,
Of straw, of string; and, at all hours,
One hears your dry haughty laugh break out
And with each peal suspend the blackbirds' baroque cadence
And likewise the sparrows' effervescent talk.
The morning concert will become quite concise
When your family passes from two to five
And the courtyard, already subject to raucous doves,
Resounds from its quarrels' endless noise.
It's true that in the heraldry of animals,
Nothing outdoes the sobriety of the two colors
That, drawing yours from sable and pure silver,
Make you recognizable among a thousand others,
Like this flight with its mechanical roll, heavy,
That seems to imitate a kite's uneven sway.
Some, well before me, admiring your aplomb,
Said you walked in evening gowns,
Elegant and sly as Lupin has been depicted,
That other coveter of glitter.
For you're known moreover to be larcenous, mean,
And you really sing too poorly for me to sing
Your praise differently than I do. Thus it would be better,
Pestering pie, that you quickly turn deserter,
Before a less calm local plans
To persuade you to go with his carbine.

UN PARADIS D'OISEAUX

Dans ce dédale froid de cours intérieures,
Le platane, l'érable et divers arbrisseaux
Composent un sous-bois, des voûtes, des berceaux
Où dès le mois d'avril, entre cinq et six heures,
On s'éveille au milieu d'un paradis d'oiseaux.

Sans compter les corbeaux, les geais, ni cette pie
Dont la gorge n'émet qu'un âpre grincement
Et qui cherchent parfois ailleurs un logement
Plus conforme aux besoins de leur misanthropie,
Mille voix avec le soleil vont s'enflammant.

Sous la pivoine encore sombre de l'aurore
Qui penche vers les fronts encore obscurs, j'entends
Ces appels des oiseaux, d'abord intermittents
Transformer tout l'espace en diamant sonore
Croisant ses feux au coeur immobile du temps.

S'il me fallait imaginer celui des anges
Et situer son apogée en quelque endroit,
Je prendrais ce concert et son beau désarroi
De grives, de pinsons, de merles, de mésanges,
Qui d'instant en instant se complique, s'accroît,

Et le verrais ainsi dans un quadrilatère
Paisible sous le dôme étincelant du ciel,
Avec un vent léger qui fait torrentiel
Le feuillage nouveau recouvrant le mystère
D'un dieu voluptueux et confidentiel.

A PARADISE OF BIRDS

In this cold maze of inner courtyards, the mix
Of plane, maple and various shrubs
Forms an undergrowth, bowers, vaults,
Where as of April, between five and six,
One wakes amidst a paradise of birds.

Not counting the crows, the jays, or this magpie
Whose throat emits only a harsh grating
That sometimes seek elsewhere housing
More consonant with the needs of their misanthropy,
A thousand light voices accompany the sun exalting.

Under the dawn's still dark peony
That leans toward the still mysterious faces, I hear
These birds' cries, at first irregular
Transform all space into a diamond resonating sweetly
Crossing its fires in time's motionless heart.

If I had to imagine that of the angels
And situate its apogee in a particular place,
I'd take this concert and its sweet disarray
Of thrushes, chaffinches, titmice, blackbirds,
Which with each instant thickens, increases,

And would see it thus in a peaceful quadrilateral
Under the sky's sparkling dome,
With a slight wind that brings home
The mystery of a god, voluptuous, confidential,
That the torrential new foliage wants to make known.

Mais entre les plus étonnantes des vocalistes,
J'ai remarqué, depuis trois ou quatre matins,
Les arpèges hardis, les trilles argentins
De deux merles ardents comme des duellistes ;
Auprès d'eux les rayons du jour semblent éteints.

Rivalisant d'éclat pendant une heure entière,
Virtuoses mais inspirés, ne rabâchant
Jamais, ils font briller à la fois le tranchant
D'une lame et le bloc d'idéale matière
D'où s'élèvent les jets capricieux du chant.

Et si fort et si librement qu'ils s'évertuent,
On les sait asservis aux lois de la saison.
Mais par l'accouplement et par la couvaison,
C'est encore leur chant qu'ils aiment, perpétuent,
À la folle hauteur de ce diapason.

C'est parfois si tendu, si plein, qu'on appréhende
Et qu'on espère aussi les entendre soudain,
Dans un vague demi-sommeil presque enfantin,
Se déchirer sur une ouverture béante
Qui nous rendrait le paradis, en ce jardin.

But among the most surprising vocalists,
I noticed, three or four mornings ago,
The silvery trills, the bold arpeggios
Of two blackbirds ardent as duelists;
Compared to them the day's rays have no glow.

Rivals in brilliance for an entire hour,
Virtuoso yet inspired, never repeating,
They bring a gleam both to the cutting
Edge of a blade and the block of ideal matter
From which rise the whimsical streams of song.

And however loud and freely they strive,
One knows they're enslaved to the laws of the season.
But through mating and through incubation,
It's again their song that they love, keep alive,
At the tremendous height of this diapason.

It's sometimes so taut, so full, that one grasps
And one hopes to also suddenly hear them,
In a vague half-sleep like that of children,
Tear through a gaping gap
That would give us back paradise, in this garden.

UNE THÉBAÏDE

Le vernis du Japon, les platanes, l'érable
Ont la même façon de se tenir dans l'air :
Tous se sont élancés vers le ciel désirable,
Étageant lentement leurs nappes de flot vert.

En bas, une herbe pauvre et quelques graminées;
Dans l'intervalle, un beau lilas et des tilleuls :
Je vis au fond du lac entre des cheminées,
Furtif et diligent comme les campagnols.

C'est un bout de papier, vierge ou non, que je ronge;
Quelquefois la journée y passe, peu ou prou,
Et de rat je me sens devenir une oronge,
Mais la clarté descend aux abords de ce trou.

Jaune et bleue, à travers les feuilles qui m'effacent
Et qu'agitent sans fin de vagues tourbillons,
Elle m'offre un poème écrit par la surface
Invisible là-haut à force de rayons.

Je ne comprends pas bien comment, dans cette écluse,
Le vent peut s'introduire et jouer sous les eaux.
Mais toujours un courant dans la masse confuse
Semble vibrer avec les ailes des oiseaux,

Avec l'or tamisé qui croule en cataracte
Le long de la fenêtre où je reviens m'asseoir
Devant ma page et mon silence où se réfracte
L'excessive beauté du monde, jusqu'au soir.

A SOLITARY RETREAT

The varnish tree, the planes, the maple
Have the same way of holding themselves in the air:
All have thrust themselves toward the desirable
Sky, slowly setting in tiers their sheets of green waves.

Below, sparse grass and a few graminae;
In between, a handsome lilac and lindens:
I live between vents deep within the lake,
Furtive and diligent like the voles.

It's a bit of paper, blank or not, that I consume;
Sometimes the day passes, in part, in whole,
And once a rat now I'm an agaric mushroom,
But the clearness comes down around this hole.

Yellow and blue, through the leaves that hide my presence,
And that vague eddies endlessly wave,
It offers me a poem written by the surface
Invisible above by dint of rays.

I don't quite understand how, in this lock,
The wind can introduce itself and, below, start playing.
But always a current in the water's muddled bulk
Seems to vibrate with the birds' wings,

With the filtered gold that tumbles in torrents
Along the window where I return to sit
Before my page and my silence where the inordinate
Beauty of the world, until evening, is refracted.

L'AUBE

À quatre heures, l'été, pas un son, pas un souffle
N'émeuvent le sommeil des arbres. Tout au bout
Des jardins, une trace irréelle de soufre
Brûle au faîte d'un toit somnambule. Debout
Dans les rideaux de cet immuable théâtre
Dont les acteurs ont l'air à jamais endormis,
J'aperçois le reflet d'une lampe bleuâtre
Se faufiler entre les troncs. Le jour promis,
Encore lent et gourd au fond de son scaphandre,
Pourrait en cet instant fragile se suspendre
À l'unique lueur qui brille sur son front
Et, comme des esprits que leur sort obnubile,
Le convoi d'arbres glisserait presque immobile
Sur le flot sans remous d'un nouvel Achéron.
Puis un, deux craquements délivrent une branche,
Un premier merle allume au loin son premier cri,
Un autre lui répond et leur flamme déclenche
De proche en proche un incendie incirconscrit.
Les feuillages alors subitement s'ébrouent
Tandis qu'au ciel le souffle d'une énorme roue
Passe.

THE DAWN

At four, in summer, neither sound nor breath
Disturbs the trees' sleep. Far back in the gardens,
An unreal trace of sulphur burns
At the top of a somnambulist roof.
Standing in the curtains of this unchanging theater
Whose actors seem forever asleep,
I see a bluish lamps's reflection worm
Its way between the trunks. Still deep
Within its spacesuit, slow and numb,
The promised day could in this fragile instant suspend
Itself on the sole glimmer that shines on its face
And, like spirits who find their fate still obsesses,
The procession of trees would glide nearly motionless
On the unswirling tide of a new Acheron's trace.
Then one, two crackles deliver a branch,
A first blackbird lights up far off its first cry,
Another answers, their flame soon launches
Step by step an uncontained fire.
The leaves then suddenly shake themselves
While in the sky the breath of a great wheel
Passes.

LA DEUXIÈME CHAMBRE

L'érable qui frémit devant notre fenêtre
Est comme une autre chambre où nous ne pénétrons
Qu'au moment de dormir et dans les environs
Du rêve, quand il est malaisé de connaître
Ce qui distingue l'âme et le corps, et la nuit.
Alors nous devenons peu à peu ce feuillage
Qui chuchote sans cesse et peut-être voyage
Avec notre sommeil qu'il héberge et conduit
Dans la profondeur même où les racines plongent,
Où vague sous le vent le sommet des rameaux.
Nous dormons, l'arbre veille, il écoute les mots
Que murmure en dormant l'arbre confus des songes.

THE SECOND ROOM

The maple that trembles in front of our window
Is like another room we enter
Only when falling asleep and near
Dreams, when it's difficult to know
What distinguishes the soul and the body, and the night.
Then we become little by little this foliage
That endlessly whispers and perhaps travels
With our sleep which it takes in and leads right
To where roots plunge, the very depths,
Where the top of small branches wanders under the wind.
We sleep, the tree keeps watch, it listens to the words
The dark tree of dreams murmurs as it sleeps.

LA POÉSIE

Est-il un seul endroit de l'espace ou du temps
Où l'un des mille oiseaux qui sont les habitants
De ce poème (ou lui, consentant, leur otage),
Entendrait quelque chose enfin de son langage
    Un peu comme je les entends,

Si peu distincts du pépiement de la pensée
Indolente, prodigue et souvent dispersée
Au fond de je ne sais quel feuillage de mots,
Que mes rimes, pour y saisir une pincée
    De sens, miment ces animaux?

J'ai supposé parfois une suprême oreille
À qui cette volière apparaîtrait pareille,
Dans l'inintelligible émeute de ses cris,
À celle dont je crois être, lorsque j'écris,
    Un représentant qui s'effraye

Et s'enchante à la fois de tant d'inanité.
Il se peut en effet que l'on soit écouté
Et qu'en un certain point le latin du poète,
Mêlé de rossignol, hulotte ou gypaète,
    Les égale en limpidité.

POETRY

Is there a single place in space or time
Where one of the thousand birds that inhabit
This poem (or it, consenting, their hostage)
Would finally hear something of its language
    A bit like I hear them,

So little distinct from the chirping of prodigious
Indolent thought often dispersed
Deep within I don't know what foliage of words,
That my rhymes, to seize there a pinch
    Of sense, mimic these birds?

At times I've imagined a supreme ear
To whom this aviary would appear
The same, in the murky riot of its cries,
As that of which I feel I am, when I write,
    A representative who fears

And also delights in so much that's inane.
Indeed it may be that someone listens
And that some Latin of the writer,
Mixed with nightingale, tawny owl or bearded vulture,
    Is equally clear, calm, serene.

LES MARTEAUX

Le matin, quand j'écris des vers silencieux
Qui ressemblent à ceux que j'aurais aimé lire,
Et que les passereaux, de leur menu délire,
M'encouragent, parfois trois ou quatre messieurs

S'installent dans la cour avec scie et marteaux
Et, cachés par la masse heureuse de l'érable,
Se disposent à faire un bruit considérable,
Sans grands égards pour mes desseins transcendentaux.

J'ignore la raison pratique de ces coups
Sonnant jusqu'au moment béni du casse-croûte
Et qui devraient en peu de temps mettre en déroute
Ma rêverie avec ses outils et ses clous

Délicats. Cependant c'est en juin, tous les sons
Prennent une épaisseur elle-même songeuse
Où la mémoire ainsi qu'une lente plongeuse
S'enfonce toujours plus avant. Puis nous glissons

De lueur en lueur, comme dans un sous-bois,
Au rythme régulier de ces clous dans des planches,
Et soudain le soleil sur les façades blanches
Fait briller un matin plein d'oiseaux d'autrefois.

THE HAMMERS

Mornings, when I write silent verse
That resembles what I would have liked to read,
And when the sparrows, in slight frenzy, seem to plead
For more, at times three or four sirs

Set up in the courtyard with saw and hammers
And, hidden by the maple's happy mass,
Prepare to make considerable noise and fuss,
Without great care for my transcendental intentions.

I'm unaware of the practical reason for these blasts
Ringing out up to the solemn sandwich time
And that should shortly, disconcertingly, divert my mind
From its reverie with its delicate tools

And nails. Nonetheless it's June, all sounds
Take on a thickness itself dreamy
Where like a slow diver memory
Plunges ever further on. Then we slide

From glimmer to glimmer, as within a wood,
To the regular rhythm of these nails in blocks,
And suddenly the sun on the white façades
Emblazes a morning full of yesteryear's birds.

LES ÉCLAIRS DE CHALEUR

Après un jour broyé sous un ciel d'ardoise aux
Durs reflets qui troublaient d'harmonieux oiseaux
    Crissant alors comme des craies,
En vain l'on attendit le tonnerre. Il n'y eut,
Spasmodique et muet dans cet amas feuillu,
    Qu'un vol de livides effraies,
Et des doigts échappés d'un rêve d'étrangleur
Appliquaient, arrachaient des masques de pâleur
    Et d'épouvante à nos visages.
Puis un seul tremblement énorme et continu
Saisit le corps de la lumière enfermé nu
    Dans un frais enfer de feuillages.
Mais plus tard j'entendis bruire à mon chevet
Le vieux livre du temps enfin rouvert, ses pages
    Comme un arbre neuf : il pleuvait.

THE SUMMER LIGHTNING

After a day ground to powder under a sky like gray
Slate with harsh reflections troubling birds' harmony
    As they took to grating like chalk,
In vain we awaited the thunder. There was
Only, spasmodic and mute in this leafy mass,
    A flight of leaden barn-owls,
And fingers escaped from dreams of a strangler
Applied, tore away masks of pallor
    And of dread from our faces.
Then a single huge trembling not to be stopped
Seized the light's naked body trapped
    In a fresh inferno of foliage.
But later in bed I heard rustling
Time's old book at last reopened, its pages
    Like a new tree: it was raining.

L'ORAGE

Vert et jaune le bel orage entre par la fenêtre,
Tandis que la pluie au-dehors crépite comme un feu
Dans les arbres qui dodelinent de la tête.
Et chaque branche bouge avec un mouvement d'adieu
Ou d'abandon complet à la nuit qui pénètre,
Invincible sous le couvert d'une épaisse clarté.
Bientôt plus rien ne lui résiste; elle passe outre
Aux dernières lueurs qui voudraient l'arrêter,
Et les absorbe dans sa masse où parfois une poutre
Énorme craque avec un pâle éclair déchiqueté.
Mais aussi la fraîcheur avec elle s'avance
Comme un souffle d'aube à la fin de ce jour étouffant
Et, du fond de l'orage au fond du sommeil, en silence,
Passe l'obscurité d'un pas léger d'enfant.

THE STORM

Green and yellow the fine storm enters by the window,
While the rain outside crackles like a fire
In the trees whose heads nod gently.
And each branch moves with a gesture of goodbye
Or of complete abandon to the night that passes
Through, invincible under the thick clear light.
Soon nothing more resists it; it ignores
The last glimmers that would like to stop it,
And absorbs them in its mass where at times
An enormous beam cracks with a pale jagged flash.
But also the freshness with it advances
Like a breath of dawn at the end of this day's stifled
Air and, from within the storm within sleep, in silence,
Darkness goes by with a light step like a child's.

SAISON MUETTE

Les arbres dénudés, après deux jours de pluie,
Ne portent plus qu'un ciel monotone, d'un blanc
Douteux de drap d'hôtel où leurs branches appuient
Quelques touches de rouille au bout d'un poing tremblant.

On redécouvre alors les façades qui cernent
Sous l'ardoise et le zinc l'espace de la cour
Et la transforment en une morne citerne
De silence qu'un merle en silence parcourt.

Les bruits atténués de la ville y pénètrent
Et déposent, au fond d'un seul bourdonnement
De forêt invisible où, dans chaque fenêtre,
S'entrouvre le reflet d'un long chemin dormant.

Tout en bas cependant, sous les terribles gestes
Des platanes figés pâles comme des os,
Un remous fait flotter des arbustes modestes
Dont le feuillage tisse encore des réseaux

Verts et dorés contre les murs sombres où s'offre,
Dans des recoins et sur le toit d'un cabanon,
Comme le contenu resplendissant d'un coffre,
L'or rouge et brun que pille un parti de moineaux.

Sur l'autre face des maisons qui semblent vides,
Peut-être n'y a-t-il plus rien que du désert.
Le monde s'est blotti dans ces jardins humides,
Arche d'automne en train de sombrer dans l'hiver.

MUTE SEASON

The bare trees, after two days of rain,
Wear only a monotonous sky now, a doubtful
White like hotel sheets where their branches press
A few spots of rust at the end of a trembling fist.

One rediscovers then the façades that surround
Under the slate and zinc the courtyard's space
And transform it into a doleful cistern
Of silence glanced at by a blackbird in silence.

The city's attenuated noise passes
Through and forms a sediment, within a single hum
Of invisible forest where, in each window,
The reflection of a long sleeping path half-opens.

Meanwhile further down, under the fearsome gestures
Of plane trees frozen pale like bones,
An eddy sets afloat small modest shrubs
Whose foliage weaves again green and golden

Networks against the dark walls where,
On a shed's roof and in hidden recesses,
Like the resplendent contents of a safe,
Red and brown gold appears, which a party of sparrows raids.

On the other side houses that seem empty,
Perhaps nothing's left there but desert.
The world has curled up in these humid gardens,
An autumn ark now sinking into winter.

Parfois un carreau s'ouvre : en hâte un bras secoue
Un chiffon rouge ou bleu qui bientôt disparaît
Dans une profondeur de vie où l'on échoue
À s'enfoncer, à fuir, prisonnier de l'attrait

Qu'exerce le secret insondable des autres.
Mais doucement le ciel s'éclaire; il est midi.
Et les oiseaux, craignant les branches les plus hautes,
S'appellent, clandestins, sous le jour engourdi.

At times a pane opens: in haste an arm shakes
A red or blue rag that soon disappears
In a depth of life where one fails
To sink in, to flee, a prisoner of the appeal

The unfathomable secret of others exerts.
But it's noon; gently the sky's grayness fades.
And the birds, fearing the highest branches,
Call each other, as if in secret, under the sluggish day.

LA MAISON BLANCHE

À présent que l'hiver ne laisse qu'une main
Qui fait signe au sommet désolé d'un platane,
On distingue, à travers le mince filigrane
Des branches, un immeuble entièrement repeint
D'un blanc métaphysique où la moindre moulure
Ornant chaque fenêtre au cadre sans défaut,
Révèle un ordre qui, sans tout à fait l'exclure,
Paraît indifférent à celui du cerveau.
Ce n'est pas sans rapport avec le cri d'alarme
Non moins secret du merle à l'approche du soir,
Et Dieu sait quel regret, rentré comme une larme,
Me prend quand vient l'hiver et que je peux revoir
La maison blanche – quel regret, ou quel espoir.

THE WHITE HOUSE

Now that winter leaves only a hand waving
At a plane tree's desolate top,
You can make out, through the thin filigree design
Of the branches, an entirely repainted building
In metaphysical white where the slightest wood
Molding adorning each window's flawless frame
Reveals an order that, without quite excluding it,
Appears indifferent to the mind's.
It's not unrelated to the alarmed cry
No less secret of the blackbird as evening approaches,
And God knows what regret, like a tear that's choked,
Overtakes me when I can see again the white house as
Winter comes – what regret, or what hope.

MATIN

Après l'instant où la braise du soir fulgure
(Le ciel ouvre un palais de houille et de jasmin
Aux plafonds bas, aux longs couloirs où la figure
Du temps fuyant hésite à suivre son chemin),

Je préfère celui qui précède l'aurore,
Quand la lueur qui monte au ciel oriental,
Verte, mais de ce vert où du feu s'élabore,
Brille dans les carreaux glacés de l'hôpital.

Comme si le matin envahissait les chambres
Par une baie ouverte en face sur la mer,
Pour atteindre la cour, amas d'ombre et de cendres
Où le faible rayon de ma lampe se perd.

Puis l'hôpital n'est plus qu'un haut hangar livide
Éblouissant la peur dans des cubes laqués
Au néon, sous le ciel illuminé mais vide,
Hors un ou deux oiseaux qui paraissent traqués.

Je prends ces visions du petit jour (pour fausses
Qu'elles semblent, après un court moment d'espoir)
Comme le seul accès à des métamorphoses
Qui permettraient enfin de comprendre, de voir

Ce que la nuit, le jour, même, nous dissimulent,
Et le temps qui les fait tourner obstinément
Comme une porte : le signal du crépuscule
Qui brille sans bouger dans l'entrebâillement.

MORNING

After the instant where the evening's embers flash
(The sky opens a palace of coal and jasmine
With low ceilings, with long halls where the figure
Of time fleeing hesitates to follow its path),

I prefer the one that precedes the dawn,
When the glimmer that rises in the eastern sky,
Green, but the kind where fire is elaborately drawn,
Shines in the hospital's chilly panes.

As if the morning invaded the rooms
Through an opening looking onto the sea,
To reach the courtyard, a mass of shadow and ash
Where my lamp's weak light loses brilliance.

Then the hospital is only a high pallid warehouse
Dazzling fear in cubes lacquered with neon,
Under a sky now illuminated but empty
Except for one or two birds with a hunted air.

I take these early morning visions (false as
They may seem, after a brief moment of hope)
To be the only access to metamorphoses
That would allow to finally comprehend, to see,

What the night, the day, even, hides from us,
And time which makes them turn obstinately
Like a door: the signal of the dusk
That shines without moving in the half-openness.

LA GRIVE

Ainsi, comme l'oiseau qui chante sur la branche,
Ivre de la douceur subite de l'hiver,
Du fond de cette chambre où, seul, je me retranche,
Peut-être ai-je capté, modulé vers à vers,
Le signal inaudible émis par l'univers
Et dont partout la source éternelle s'épanche.

Cette grive, là-haut, croit le moment venu
De chanter. Mais savoir si c'est elle qui chante,
Ou le moment qui veut son chant discontinu,
Toujours repris, quand on la voit si diligente
Apporter entre deux silences sa tranchante
Et fervent réponse au vouloir inconnu?

Dites-moi ce qui chante à travers cette grive,
Pour que j'entende mieux enfin ce que j'écris,
Ce que la mer chuchote au long de chaque rive,
Le vent au bout de chaque rue, et tous les cris
Perdus avec les faux printemps qui m'ont surpris
Entre deux continents de neige qui dérivent.

THE THRUSH

Thus, like the bird that sings on the branch,
Drunk with the sudden gentleness of winter,
Within this room where, alone, I'm shut in, entrenched,
Perhaps I've captured, modulated verse to verse,
The inaudible signal put out by the universe
And whose eternal source everywhere flows forth.

This thrush, up above, thinks the moment has come
To sing. But as far as knowing whether the thrush sings,
Or the moment that wants the song broken,
Always resumed, when one sees how it brings
Diligence, this thrush, and between two silences its strong
And fervent answer to a will that's unknown?

Tell me what sings through this bird,
That I might better finally hear what I write,
What the sea whispers along each shore,
The wind at the end of each street, and all the cries
Lost with the false springs that surprised
Me between two continents of snow changing course.

UN INTERMÈDE À SAINT-JOSEPH

Voici l'autre côté pour moi qui, d'habitude,
Distingue entre des fleurs le mur de la maison
Douloureuse. Je vais avec ma solitude
Entre des murs s'ouvrant parfois sur un gazon
Fleuri pour honorer une pâle statue
Virginale aux deux mains capables de guérir,
Dans l'âme de celui qui prie et s'évertue,
L'ennui d'être soi-même et la peur de mourir.
Mais nous sommes si peu de chose que, sans doute,
Il ne vaut même pas la peine d'y penser.
Je veux être pareil au merle que j'écoute,
Qui l'ignore, ou s'en moque, et paraît plus sensé
Que moi qui m'imagine un peu centre du monde
(Ésotérique, non : plutôt sentimental)
Et m'en cherche une preuve à travers l'hôpital
Où je reprends encore un coup la même ronde
De galerie en véranda désertes. M'y rejoint
Après la pluie un sourd reflet du soir de juin
Qui ne veut pas finir bien que la cloche tinte
De quart d'heure en quart d'heure, inexorablement,
Mais avec la douceur même de chaque teinte
En train de fondre dans la nuit. En m'endormant,
Que cette paix longtemps encore m'enveloppe
Et que, jusqu'à ce coeur indécis qui galope,
Hésite, elle pénètre, et se répande aussi,
Tandis qu'un dernier cri du merle se syncope,
Sur tous ceux qui déjà rêvent, meurent ici.

AN INTERLUDE AT SAINT-JOSEPH

Here's the other side for me who, usually,
Makes out among flowers the grievous house's
Wall. I go with my aloneness
Between walls sometimes opening onto lawns
Adorned with flowers to honor a pale virginal
Statue with two hands able to cure,
In the soul of those who pray and strive,
The struggle of being oneself and dying's fear.
But we're of such little importance that clearly
It's not worth giving it any thought.
I want to be like the blackbird I hear,
Who is unaware, or doesn't care, and would appear
Sensible, unlike me imagining myself center of the world
(Esoteric, no: more sentimental)
And seeking proof through the hospital
Where I have another go at my rounds
Of deserted galleries and verandas. I'm joined
After the rain by the June evening's muted reflection
That doesn't want to end though the bell sounds
From each quarter of an hour to the next, inexorably,
But with the very gentleness of each tint
That's melting now into night. When I sleep,
May this peace a long while yet envelop
Me and, up to this indecisive heart that gallops,
Hesitates, may it enter, and also spread right
Through, while the blackbird emits a last syncopated
Cry for all those here who already dream, die.

LES COUVREURS

Le bleu de juin, le bleu tendre, le bleu de cendre
Qui déteint dans les yeux et jusque sur les doigts,
Le bleu fait silence entre deux mésanges sur les toits
Et contraint la rumeur sournoise à redescendre
Parmi des souffles engourdis comme dans un sous-bois.
Ce n'est plus maintenant qu'un torrent qui s'éloigne,
Presque à sec au fond des ravins divisant la montagne
Où tels des bergers deux couvreurs hèlent à pleine voix.
Et soudain je les vois, en gros pantalon et casquette,
Qui vont indifférents aux gouffres sur le faîte,
Une corde à la main qu'ils balancent, hé, ho,
Comme s'ils menaient l'attelage du soleil déjà haut.

THE ROOFERS

The blue of June, the soft blue, the ash blue
That runs off into one's eyes and as far as one's fingers,
Blue holds silent between two titmice on the roofs
And compels the hum in its stealth to come back down to
Breaths sluggish as in a thick wood.
It's now only a torrent that drifts off and away,
Almost dried up within mountain ravines that divide
Where like shepherds two roofers shout at the top of their lungs.
And suddenly I see them, in big pants and hats,
Walking indifferently along the rooftop chasms,
A rope in hand that they toss, heads up,
As if leading the sun's team already high up.

ENCORE UN SOIR

Et de nouveau les longs rayons horizontaux du soir
Se cassant en cascade éclaboussent le coeur de l'arbre.
Peut-être est-ce le seul instant où l'on pourrait les voir
Reposer au coeur de l'année. En tout cas ils s'attardent
Et leur flot de plus en plus dense à mesure suspend
Son or parmi les jets éblouissants de cette grive
Qui reprennent comme un sanglot d'allégresse du temps,
Mais encore interrogateurs, toujours sur le qui-vive.
Roule, tendre et lourd char de roses le long des toits;
Barque lumineuse, descends les ombreuses rivières.
La rançon de tant de beauté, c'est qu'elle passe (moi
Je l'accepte, comme le soir renonce à la lumière).

ANOTHER EVENING

And again the evening's long horizontal rays
Breaking in cascades splash the tree's heart.
Perhaps it's the only moment they may
Be seen resting in the heart of the year. In any case they linger
And their ever denser flow suspends
Its gold amid this thrush's dazzling bursts
That pick up again like a sob of time's lightness,
But still questioning, always on the alert.
Go, sweet heavy chariot of roses along the roofs;
Luminous bark, descend the rivers full of night.
The price for so much beauty is that it passes (I do
Accept, as the evening renounces light).